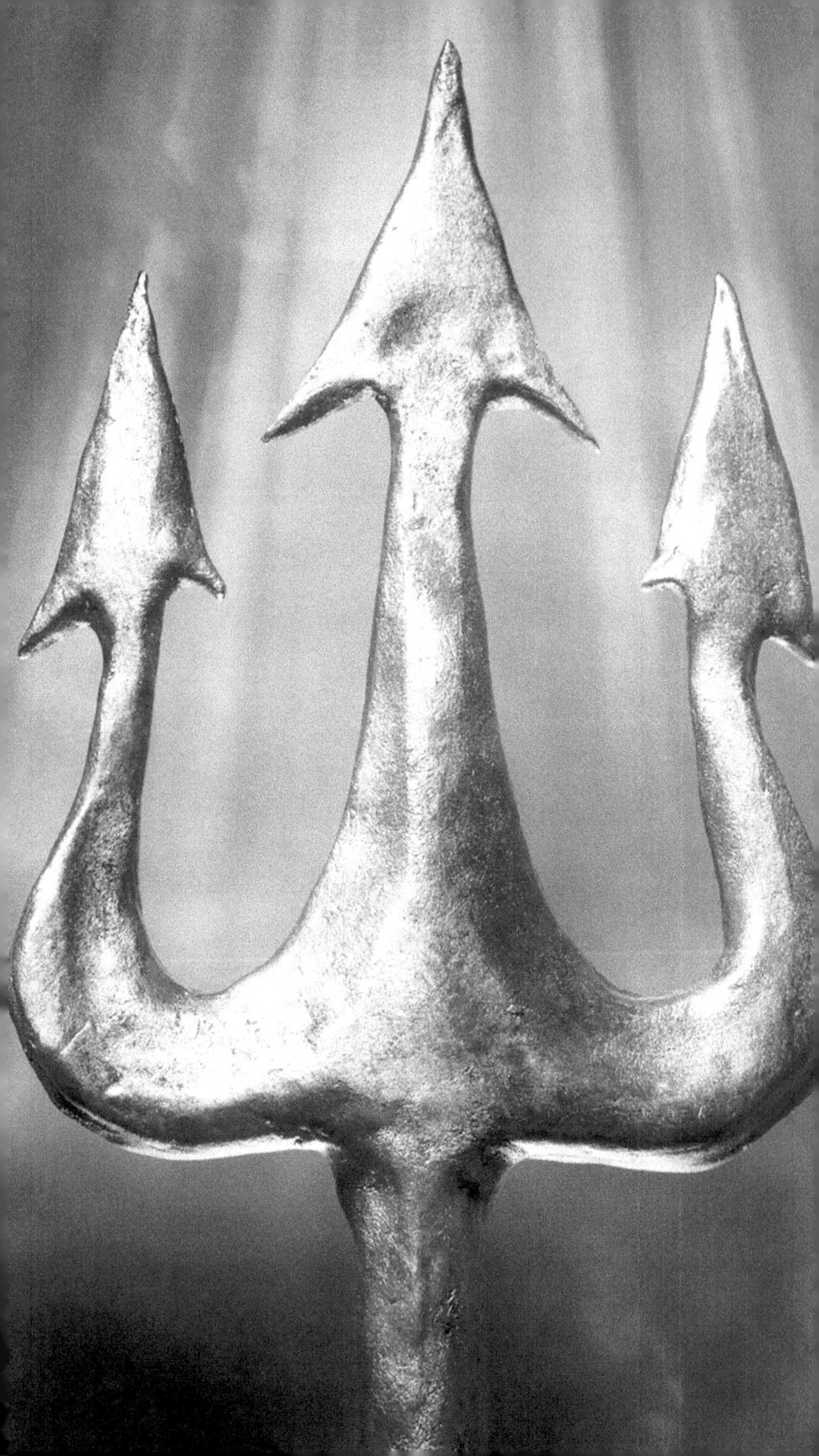

NOT
Negotiable

Trident Security Book 4

SAMANTHA COLE

To my beautiful cousin, Ginger, who passed away after a four-year battle with inoperable lung cancer while I was writing this book.

Forty-five years with you in my life was not long enough.
XOXO

AUTHOR'S NOTE

The story within these pages is completely fictional but the concepts of BDSM are real. If you do choose to participate in the BDSM lifestyle, please research it carefully and take all precautions to protect yourself. Fiction is based on real life but real life is *not* based on fiction. Remember-Safe, Sane and Consensual!

***While not every character is in every book, these are the ones with the most mentions throughout the series. This guide will help keep readers straight about who's who.

Trident Security (TS) is a private investigative and military agency co-owned by Ian and Devon Sawyer. With governmental and civilian contracts, the company started when the brothers and a few of their teammates from SEAL Team Four retired to the private sector. The company is located on a guarded compound, which was a former import/export company cover for a drug trafficking operation in Tampa, Florida. Three warehouses on the property were converted into large apartments, the TS offices, a gym, and bunk rooms.

In addition to the security business, a fourth warehouse now houses an elite BDSM club, co-owned by Devon, Ian, and their cousin, Mitch Sawyer, the manager. Much time and money has made The

Covenant the most sought-after membership in the Tampa/St. Petersburg area and beyond. Members are thoroughly vetted before being granted access to the elegant club.

Over twenty Doms have been appointed Dungeon Masters (DMs), and they rotate two or three shifts each throughout the month. At least four DMs are always on duty at various posts in the pit and play-rooms, with an additional one roaming around. Their job is to ensure the safety of all the submissives in the club. They step in if a sub uses their safeword and the Dom in the scene doesn't hear or heed it, and ensure the equipment used in scenes isn't harming the subs.

The Covenant's security team takes care of everything that isn't scene-related, provides safety for all members, and are essentially the bouncers. The current total membership is just over 350. The fire marshal had approved them for 500 when the warehouse-turned-kink club first opened, but the cousins had intentionally kept that number down to maintain elite status.

Between Trident Security and The Covenant, there's plenty of romance, suspense, and steamy encounters. Come meet the Sexy Six-Pack, their friends, family, and teammates.

The Sexy Six-Pack (Alpha Team)
and Their Significant Others

- Ian "Boss-man" Sawyer: Devon and Nick's brother; retired Navy SEAL; co-owner of Trident Security and The Covenant; fiancé/Dom of Angie.
- Devon "Devil Dog" Sawyer: Ian and Nick's brother; retired Navy SEAL; co-owner of Trident Security and The Covenant; fiancé/Dom of Kristen.
- Ben "Boomer" Michaelson: retired Navy SEAL; explosives and ordnance specialist; son of Rick and Eileen, fiancé/Dom of Katerina (Kat).
- Jake "Reverend" Donovan: retired Navy SEAL; Dom and Whip Master at The Covenant.
- Brody "Egghead" Evans: retired Navy SEAL; computer specialist; Dom.
- Marco "Polo" DeAngelis: retired Navy SEAL; communications specialist and back up helicopter pilot; Dom.
- Nick Sawyer: Ian and Devon's brother; current Navy SEAL.
- Kristen "Ninja-girl" Sawyer: author of romance/suspense novels; fiancée/submissive of Devon.
- Angelina "Angie/Angel" Sawyer: graphic artist, fiancée/submissive of Ian.
- Katerina "Kat" Michaelson: dog trainer for

law enforcement and private agencies; fiancée/submissive of Boomer.

Extended Family, Friends, and Associates of the Sexy Six-Pack

- Mitch Sawyer: Cousin of Ian, Devon, and Nick; co-owner/manager of The Covenant, Dom.
- T. Carter: US spy and assassin; works for covert agency Deimos; Dom.
- Shelby Whitman: human resource clerk; two-time cancer survivor; submissive.
- Parker Christiansen: owner of New Horizons Construction; Dom.
- Curt Bannerman: retired Navy SEAL; owner of Halo Customs, a motorcycle repair and detail shop.
- Jenn "Baby-girl" Mullins: college student; goddaughter of Ian; "niece" of Devon, Brody, Jake, Boomer, and Marco; father was a Navy SEAL; parents murdered.
- Mike Donovan: owner of the Irish pub, Donovan's; brother of Jake.
- Charlotte "Mistress China" Roth: Parole officer; Domme and Whip Master at The Covenant.
- Travis "Tiny" Daultry: former professional football player; head of security at The

Covenant and Trident compound; occasional bodyguard for TS.

- Rick and Eileen Michaelson: Boomer's parents. Rick is a retired Navy SEAL.
- Charles "Chuck" and Marie Sawyer: Ian, Devon, and Nick's parents. Charles is a self-made real estate billionaire. Marie is a plastic surgeon involved with Operation Smile.
- Will Anders: Assistant Curator of the Tampa Museum of Art Kristen Anders's cousin.
- Dr. Roxanne London: pediatrician; Domme/wife (Mistress Roxy) of Kayla.
- Kayla London: social worker; submissive/wife of Roxanne.
- Chase Dixon: retired Marine Raider; owner of Blackhawk Security; associate of TS.
- Doug Henderson: retired Marine; bodyguard.
- Reggie Helm: lawyer for TS and The Covenant; boyfriend/Dom of Colleen.
- Colleen McKinley: office manager of TS; girlfriend/submissive of Reggie.
- Carl Talbot: college professor; Dom and Whip Master at The Covenant.

Members of Law Enforcement

- Larry Keon: Assistant Director of the FBI.
- Frank Stonewall: Special Agent in Charge of the Tampa FBI.
- Calvin Watts: Leader of the FBI HRT in Tampa.

The K9s of Trident

- Beau: An orphaned Lab/Pit mix, rescued by Ian. Now a trained K9 who has more than earned his spot on the Alpha Team.

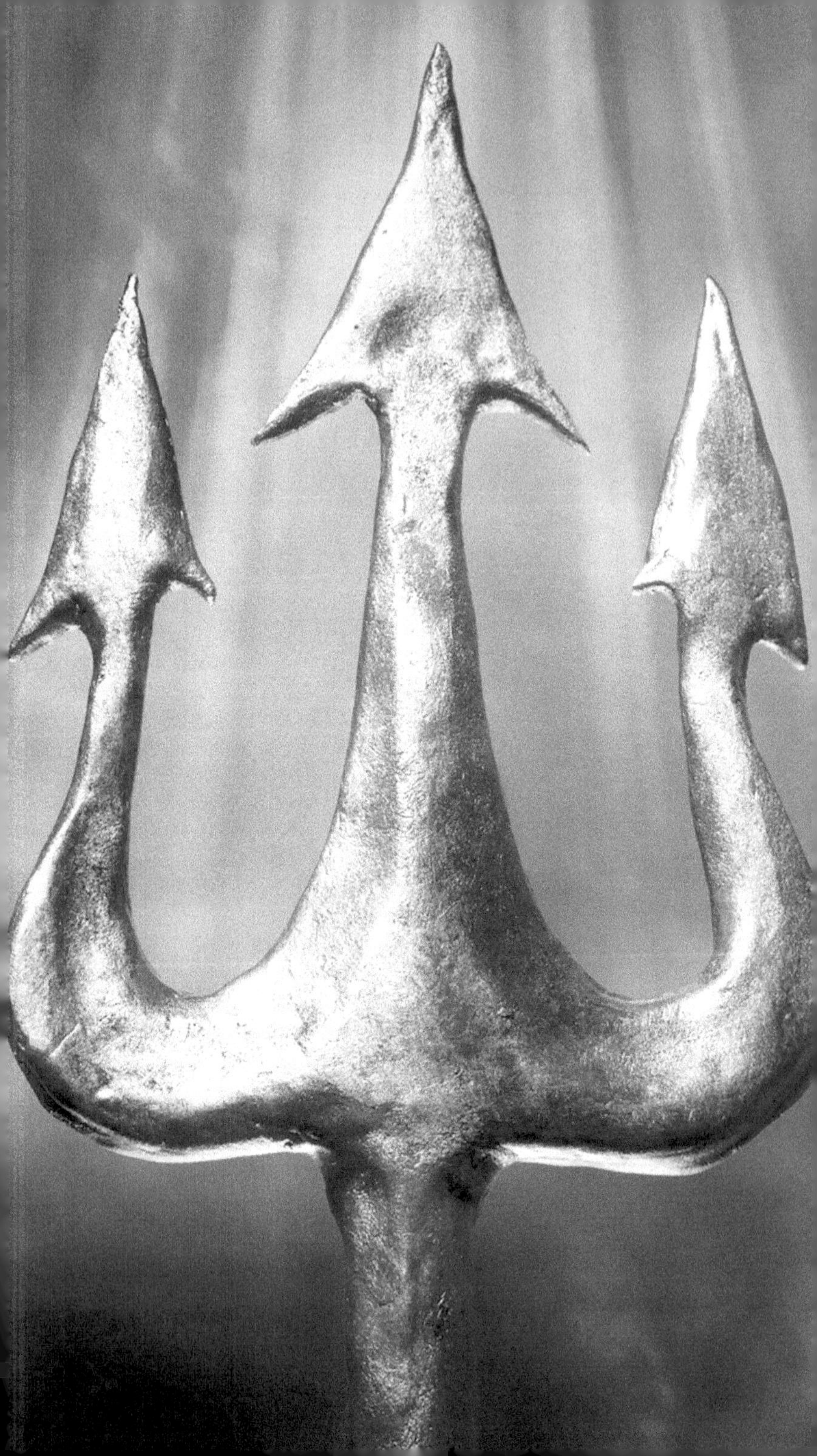

CHAPTER ONE

Mentally rolling his eyes, Parker Christiansen listened as his older brother droned on about life in Boston—a life Parker felt he never fit into and had left behind years ago. Dave was just like their parents—stuck-up, arrogant, and rich. He'd even followed in their father's footsteps and became a successful corporate attorney.

Meanwhile, Parker had taken his love for using his hands to build things and become an architect/builder/contractor. And no matter how successful he'd made his company, New Horizons, his father always managed to put him down. Nothing he ever did was good enough for the old man. Their family came from wealth and privilege, and Judge Alan and Janet Christiansen couldn't accept that their youngest son liked getting his hands dirty. They also didn't like that Parker was a Dom in the BDSM lifestyle—a fact

Alan had found out by accident several years ago—and he never let his son forget it.

But his brother had always been curious about the lifestyle—not in front of their parents, of course. Dave had called him a few weeks ago, saying he would be in Florida on business this weekend, and he wanted Parker to bring him as a guest to the club he belonged to. The Covenant was a private and elite BDSM club in Tampa, and Parker had been a member since the doors opened over four years ago. His company had done some of the work on the club, as well as the other three warehouses in the gated compound.

He had converted one of the buildings into two apartments for the club's owners, Ian and Devon Sawyer, and was in the process of adding two more apartments in the currently unused half of the building. From what he was told, Ian's goddaughter, Jenn, was getting one, while their younger brother would be given the keys to the last unit for when he retired from the Navy. One of the other buildings was home to the Sawyers' company, Trident Security. The ex-Navy SEALs had a thriving business in both ventures, but their cousin Mitch Sawyer was the third co-owner and manager of the club. The club Parker and Dave were en route to.

Parker had given Mitch his brother's name to get him cleared to be a guest. The Covenant was extremely strict with running background checks on potential members and visitors. Legally binding privacy contracts had to be signed to ensure what happened at the club stayed at the club.

"Why do you want to check out the club again? I thought Carol was against the lifestyle."

Dave shrugged. "She agreed our marriage needs a little spicing up. I'm thinking about joining a club outside Boston, but I wanted to check one out first with you so you can fill me in on the lifestyle a little more."

Pulling off the highway, Parker drove down the private road leading to the compound. "Take your license out. You need to show it to the guard."

"There's a guard?"

"Yeah. The Sawyers take the security here seriously." He took the ID his brother handed him, rolled down the window, and gave it to the guard. "Hey, Murray. What are you doing here? Thought you only worked days."

The burly, armed guard swiped the license through his hand-held computer, compared the picture and name to the approved list, and then handed the card back to Parker. "Just grabbing a little overtime. One of the guys called in sick. You're all cleared. Have a good night."

"Thanks. You, too."

Parker found a spot for his truck and killed the ignition. "Give me your cell phone."

"Why?" Despite his question, Dave handed him the device.

"They aren't allowed on the floor of the club." Well, they were if they remained in a pocket or purse. Any texting or talking on phones had to be done in the lobby or parking lot. But Parker didn't want his brother to be tempted to use it inside. He tossed the phone, along with his own, into the glove compartment. "All right. Remember. I'm responsible for you here. At the front desk, you'll get a yellow wristband that indicates you're a guest and not available for play. You don't do anything without checking with me first. When I introduce you to anyone, you ask permission from the Doms or Dommes to speak to their submissives. There's a two-drink limit for guests and anyone who is going to play. Don't ask for more than that because they keep track."

Waving him off, Dave climbed out of the Chevy Tahoe. "I got it. I read all the stuff you sent in the email. No worries."

Despite his brother's assurance, Parker still couldn't help but think this was a big mistake.

Shelby Whitman walked out into the main room of the club and let the pulsating music flow through her body. Ian's new submissive seemed nice. When they'd met a few minutes ago in the women's locker room, Angie appeared nervous, but that was expected for a sub's first time in a BDSM club. Shelby hoped she'd eased the woman's anxiety with her little pep talk.

Taking a quick glance down her body, Shelby grinned at her new outfit. Tonight's color was electric blue. Her bra, mini-skirt, which flared out when she turned, and wig, with straight hair to her shoulders, all matched perfectly. What had started as a way to hide her thinning hair from radiation treatments years ago had become a fashion statement that had remained long after her treatments for ovarian cancer were completed. Now cancer-free for six years, she still wore a different colored wig to match her outfit every time she came to the club.

Glancing around, she tried to tell herself she wasn't looking for *him*, but her gaze still searched for those gentle brown eyes and blond crewcut. There were plenty of single, hot Doms at The Covenant, but something about Parker Christiansen always drew her in, making her libido wake up and take notice. Totally drool-worthy, he was continually tan from working outside. She knew he owned his building company. However, he wasn't the type of guy to sit behind a desk and let others do the dirty work. Parker got right down in the trenches with his employees.

But the Dom wasn't for her. He needed more than a submissive... he needed a wife. Parker was the type of guy who should grow old with the woman he loved, spoiling lots of children and grandchildren. Something Shelby could never give him. It was part of the reason why she liked the lifestyle—well, besides the incredible orgasms she tended to receive regularly from any of the other single Doms who wanted to play. She could hook up with anyone who wasn't looking for long-term... anyone who only wanted a relationship here at the club and not out in the "real" world.

Before her cancer, she had wanted a long-term relationship with a Dom/husband, two-point-six kids, a dog, and a house with a white picket fence. But that was before fate had been cruel. Now, she had nothing to offer a man except sex and friendship. So, she came here, put on her best smile and the bouncy personality everyone loved, before going home... alone.

Taking a deep breath, she pushed Master Parker from her mind and headed to the submissives' waiting area. Maybe Masters Brody and Marco would be here and willing to indulge her in one of their ménages. The two always left her sated and well-cared for without emotional attachments. And that was just fine with her.

*****

An hour after they arrived, Parker was dying to get out of there. It wasn't that he didn't want to be at the club—he just didn't want to be there with his brother. He knew this had been a mistake. While Dave had been asking a bunch of questions, it was apparent he still had no clue about the lifestyle and didn't belong in it. It was also pissing the Dom off that his brother was leering at every scantily dressed sub that walked by as if she were a piece of meat. Having him here was a recipe for disaster.

In addition to his brother issues, he didn't want to watch Shelby's scene with the Masters of Ménage. Brody Evans and Marco DeAngelis were the popular tag-team duo for the female submissives, and a few minutes ago, he'd watched from afar as Shelby and the two Doms negotiated a scene. Well, mostly, Brody did the negotiating with the blonde sub. Marco was on Dungeon Master duty at the moment and had kept one ear on the other two and his eyes on everything else going on around him. The DMs were all experienced Doms or Dommes who took shifts to ensure no harm came to any submissive, whether intentional or not. And Parker was one of them.

Forcing himself to stop mooning over Shelby, who was chatting with a few other people in a sitting area designated for submissives, he bit his lip in frustration. She was probably waiting for Marco to get off his scheduled shift. Parker glanced at his watch. The DM would be free in about fifteen minutes. "Hey, Dave. Since you can't play and I can't leave you alone, why don't we go somewhere else and have a few drinks."

His brother tilted his head. "I'm fine here, but if you want, we can sit upstairs, have a few drinks, and watch from one of the balcony tables."

Not the response he wanted, but at least they'd be out of the "pit," as the members called the huge downstairs playroom. The entrance was on the second floor, where the bar was. The U-shaped balcony had numerous seating areas, with some along the railing so members could observe the scenes from above. He could pick the side over the spanking benches so he wouldn't have to watch Shelby's threesome and dream she was his submissive—and his alone. He'd tried to negotiate with her twice in the past, and she'd turned him down both times. It was a single submissive's prerogative to play or not play with whomever they wanted, and a Dom had to accept it. He only wished he knew why she wanted nothing to do with him.

Parker stood. "Yeah, that's fine. Let's take a walk through the locker rooms. I need to hit the john."

Their table was not far from the submissives' waiting area, halfway between the grand staircase and the St. Andrew's cross on a small stage in the middle of the room. Usually, the stage was reserved for high-lighted scenes or commitment ceremonies. Devon and his sub/fiancée, Kristen Anders, had their ceremony on it a few months ago, and Parker was glad his friend had finally found someone to love. He only hoped someday he could be so lucky.

Still eyeing the activity around them, his brother remained seated. "I'll wait here for you. No rush."

"I'm not supposed to leave you unattended."

Dave rolled his eyes. "Come on, Park. I'm a grown man and don't need a babysitter. I promise to wait right here."

Hesitating, Parker was about to say no way, but

Dave gave him that stare that always made him feel like the idiot of the family. That fucking holier-than-thou look that said I'm better than you'll ever be. "All right, fine. But stay here and don't talk to anyone unless they approach you first. I'll be back in a minute."

He headed to the locker room, glancing over his shoulder once at his brother. The cocky bastard gave him one of those condescending waves like he was shooing away an annoying gnat. Parker winced and disappeared into the men's lounge. In there, the sounds of flesh, or leather, smacking flesh, and orgasms being reached faded away while the thumping music was muffled enough so he could hear himself think. Why he agreed to come here tonight, he had no idea. It wasn't like he and Dave were the closest of brothers... hell, if it weren't for the blood relation, Parker wouldn't even consider him a friend. Four years younger than Dave's age of thirty-five, he had always lived in the guy's shadow. That was one of the reasons he'd moved to Florida... to get away from his family.

Brody stepped up to the urinal next to Parker. "Hey, man. How you doin'?"

"Good. You?"

"Not bad at all. Especially since little Miss Shelby negotiated a scene with Marco and me for later. Damn, I love that little firecracker."

Parker clenched his teeth. He knew Brody had

nothing but respect for the submissive. However, it irked him that the big bastard knew her in a way Parker had never experienced. The computer geek of Trident Security was a former Navy SEAL, as was each of his co-workers. He also had a heart of gold and was well-liked by everyone who met him. Brody treated every female submissive as they should be treated... like they were the most precious women in the world.

Zipping up his pants, Parker turned toward the sinks and tried to pretend it didn't bother him who Shelby hooked up with. "Well, then, have a good time."

"Hey, before I forget... can I call you during the week? I want to overhaul the master bath in my new place. Pink tile and I don't exactly go together, and the shower is way too fucking small." He finished at the urinals and stepped over to where Parker was washing his hands.

"Yeah, sure. Monday's usually a busy day, but I should have time Tuesday afternoon to swing by and take a look." Shaking the excess water from his hands, Parker reached over and grabbed a paper towel. He glanced back to see the other man was nodding.

"That should work. I'll call you Tuesday morning to confirm. Thanks. I appreciate it."

Slapping Brody on the shoulder as he walked by, he said, "No problem. See you later."

Wanting to get out of the club now more than ever, Parker strode back out to the pit, where two things hit him at once. One—his brother wasn't where he left him. And two—there was a large, loud crowd near the submissives' area, and it didn't appear to be for anything good. *Fuck!*

Shoving his way through the group, he wasn't expecting what he saw, although he wasn't too surprised. Dave was on the floor, face-down, with one arm hitched high behind his back by a furious Marco. His brother was no match for the security operative who worked out almost daily.

Parker had a sinking feeling in his stomach when he saw three women also on the floor a few feet away. Mistress China and a woman he didn't recognize had their arms around... *shit*... a crying Shelby. Wide-eyed, she held a trembling hand against her cheek while the Domme looked ready to spit nails.

With his fists clenched, he turned his attention back to the two men and barked, "What the fuck, Dave? What the hell did you do?"

"I didn't do anything. Now get this fucking gorilla off me. I'm going to sue if he doesn't get off me."

The whiny, pain-filled order didn't gain any sympathy from Parker. His gaze went to Marco, who growled and returned the questioning look with a pissed-off glower. "This asshole backhanded Shelby. I had people in my way and couldn't get here fast enough to stop him."

What? The bastard hit Shelby? My Shelby? A woman who wouldn't hurt a fly.

Parker was livid. Glancing back toward the crying submissive, his blood hit the boiling point. Through gritted teeth, he addressed the other Dom. "He's my brother. Let him up, Marco."

Marco's eyes flickered to Ian, who was standing next to Parker. Travis "Tiny" Daultry, the head of club security, and several other guards had pushed the crowd back to give the Doms some room. Ian crossed his arms and studied Parker's face. Parker knew his fury was showing, and he silently begged the owner to let him handle this. Ian didn't say a word but nodded at Marco, who let go of the bastard and stood.

As Dave got to his feet, Parker couldn't believe he was stupid enough to say, "What's the big deal? Everyone is slapping women around here, and I get in trouble for what you all are doing."

Parker took a step closer to him, his voice low and barely controlled. "You okay?"

Obviously, not realizing how pissed his brother was, the idiot grinned. "Yeah, Park, I'm fine."

"Good." Without missing a beat, he reared back and punched Dave in the face, knocking him unconscious. He ignored the round of cheers from the crowd and hurried over to Shelby, crouching down in front of her. "I'm so sorry, Shelby. It's my fault. I shouldn't have left him alone."

He helped her stand, but Mistress China and the other woman stayed by her side for support. Parker gently pulled Shelby's hand from her cheek and growled, "I'm going to kill him," when he saw the red and swollen area, which was starting to bruise. He'd known bringing the stupid prick here was a mistake, but the fact that harm had come to Shelby, of all people, had him wanting to wake his brother up so he could knock him out again.

She grabbed his forearm, her eyes pleading. "No, don't, Sir. I should have grabbed Master Marco or one of the other DMs. He was trying to negotiate with me. I saw his guest wristband and knew he wasn't allowed to play, but he wouldn't take no for an answer. When I tried to walk away, he hit me."

Parker drew her into his arms and held her momentarily while everyone else looked on. He saw Ian cock his head at Tiny, who began breaking up the crowd with the other guards. The Head Dom then spoke quietly to Parker. "Let's take this to the office. What do you want us to do with him?"

Parker didn't answer him immediately—he had a sub to take care of first. She may not be his, but for now, he was responsible for her. He could hardly hold back the anger and guilt in his voice. "Go to the ladies' lounge and put some ice on your cheek. When I'm done with Ian and my asshole brother, I'll take you home."

"You—you don't have to do that, I can drive myself." Shelby's face flushed, and her eyes avoided him. Even though her trembling seemed to ease while in his arms, it appeared she didn't want to be there.

"I need to do this, Shelby, please. I need to make sure you're okay and get home safe. This is not negotiable." He tipped her chin up with his fingers until she looked at him. "Please?"

She bit her lip but nodded her consent. Mistress China wrapped her arm around the sub's shoulder and eased her from Parker's arms. Despite being a bit of a sadist, the Domme tended to be a mother hen to the submissives. "I'll take care of her. We'll be in the lounge when you're ready."

He murmured his thanks to her while Ian spoke to the other woman with them. Parker figured she was the owner's new submissive, whom he'd heard someone mention earlier. "I'm sorry, but I have to take care of this. Please go with them and wait for me in the lounge. I'll be a few minutes."

"Yes, Sir."

The two women walked Shelby toward the locker room, and before he joined them, Marco gave Parker a heated glare he knew he deserved. He'd broken one of the club's rules—never leave a guest unattended—and the results had been devastating.

Ian asked one of the nearby waitresses to bring an ice pack to Shelby before turning to Parker, who still wanted to commit familial homicide. Handing his keys to Tiny, Parker asked, "Can you do me a favor? Toss him into my truck. And don't bother being gentle about it. He deserves every fucking bruise he gets."

The six-foot-eight, two-hundred-and-seventy-five-pound, part-time bodyguard grinned. "My plea-sure. We'll take care of him... You just make sure Miss Shelby is okay."

"I will." Parker then turned to Ian, his face filled with embarrassment, anger, and regret. "Let's get this over with."

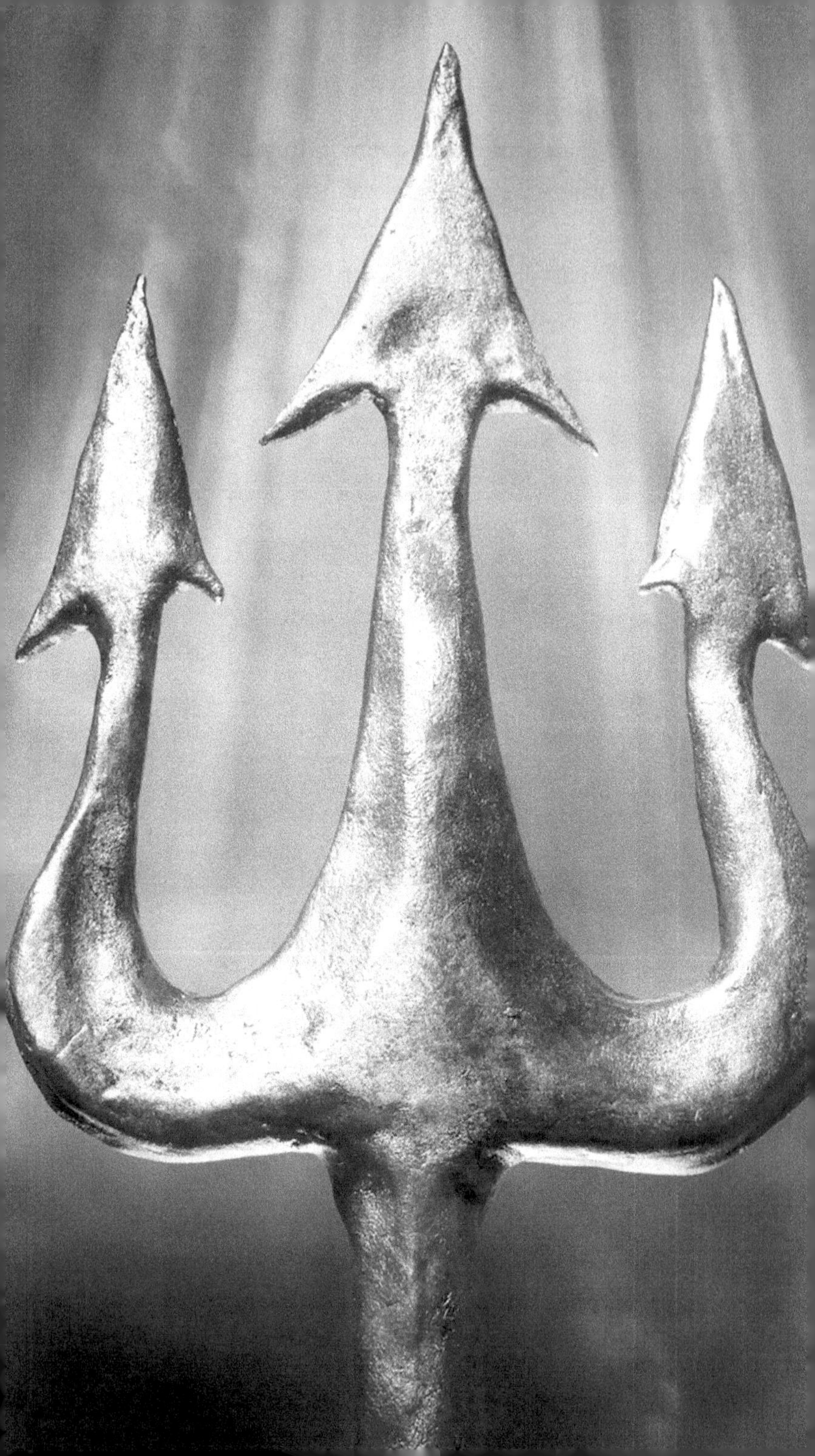

CHAPTER TWO

Parker paced behind the closed door of Mitch's office as Ian sat against the front of the desk and watched him. Usually, the manager would sit in on something like this, but Mitch was home with the flu.

Running a hand over his crewcut, Parker tried to calm down, but it was near impossible. "Fuck! I'm so sorry, Ian. I was only gone two minutes to take a fucking piss. I told him not to move from where we were sitting. He fucking knew he wasn't allowed to play or approach any subs. The only reason I even brought him here is he called me a few weeks ago and said he wanted to see the place while he was in town on business. Said he and his wife were thinking about joining a club in Boston. I knew I shouldn't have brought him here. He doesn't understand the lifestyle the way I do. I know he's cheated on his wife before, but I didn't think he was stupid enough to try something here. Fuck! I'm going to kill him."

The owner let him rant for another minute before Parker took a deep breath and glanced at him. "I broke the rules. Do what you have to do." He plopped down into one of the chairs and hung his head in defeat. He had screwed up big time and wouldn't be surprised if Ian threw him out of the club for good.

Ian crossed his arms. "I'm sorry I have to do this, but you know you're not supposed to leave a guest alone for this exact reason. You should have asked a DM or guard to watch him for the time you needed to leave him alone." Parker nodded but didn't say anything. He deserved the ass-chewing and a whole lot more. "I have to suspend your play privileges for the next twelve weeks. During that time, you'll take three DM shifts per week. I'll check the schedule and coordinate the dates and times with you tomorrow. Your guest privileges will also be suspended for two years."

Suspended? Not terminated? Thank fuck. He didn't think he could live without seeing Shelby every week, whether she agreed to play with him or not. Parker snorted. "Don't worry. I think this is the last time I'll bring anyone here, if they're in the lifestyle or not. I've learned my lesson." He dragged his hand down his face as he stood again. "I'll be back for Shelby in a few minutes. Dave's motel is about five minutes from here. I'll dump him into his room and come back. If I thought a cab would pick up the unconscious asshole, I'd call one. But since Shelby's being taken care of by China and Marco, I'll get rid of him first."

Ian nodded and followed him out of the office. At the main double doors, they separated, and Parker continued out to the lobby, where Tiny was waiting for him with his keys. As the big man tossed them to him, he gave him an impish grin. "He's all tucked in, but he may have a few bruises from when he 'accidentally' fell down a few of the stairs."

Parker smirked. "How many stairs?"

"Six or seven. Not sure. Could've been eight, but no more than nine. He might've broken his neck if that happened."

"You're the best, Tiny." He gave the head guard a fist bump. "Thanks for taking out the trash. I'll be back in a few for Shelby."

"No worries."

Exiting the front door, Parker descended the long staircase leading to the parking lot. From the outside, one would never know the building housed one of the most elite private BDSM clubs on the East Coast. It was *the* club to belong to, and Parker was lucky this wouldn't be the last time he drove out of there. Despite his anger, he couldn't help but think that this might give Shelby a chance to get to know him better and get her past whatever she had against him. As long as she didn't hate him after tonight. *Fuck!*

Shelby let Master Marco hold her while they waited in the ladies' lounge, along with Mistress China and Angie. She felt terrible that this was the new submissive's first experience in the club. Incidents like this were rare at The Covenant, but every once in a while, a jackass got through the stringent background checks.

She'd been wary when the man had approached her, immediately noticing the yellow wristband indicating he was a guest. He'd tried to convince her to meet him at his motel later—as if! When she'd tried to walk away, he grabbed her arm. And when she'd told him not too politely to fuck off, he'd backhanded her. Before she knew what was happening, Marco had him on the floor, and Angie and Mistress China were by her side.

Shelby had heard horror stories over the years about men who assumed women in the lifestyle were easy lays or, even worse—hookers. She'd even met a few of the creeps herself. It was why she never revealed that she was a member of the BDSM community unless she was certain they were members as well and not just wannabes.

Sitting on Marco's lap, she let him comfort her with softly spoken words as he ran his hand up and down her back. She knew he was not only making sure she was okay because that's what good Doms did, but taking control now was helping him deal with what had happened earlier. While she had scened with the Dom many times over the past few years, there was no romance between them, just a comfortable friendship. She didn't know much about him outside of the club other than he worked at Trident Security, but she did know he'd lost his only sister, Nina, to cancer several months ago. Many of the club's members had gone to the funeral to support him.

Shelby hoped someday Marco would find a submissive whom he could fall in love with, although he was more like her in that respect. Neither one of them believed they were able to let someone in for a long-term relationship. She wasn't sure what his reasoning was, but in her case, what man would want a woman who couldn't have kids and always lived in fear of her cancer coming back? She'd been lucky her cancer had been caught early enough, but so had Nina's. Unfortunately, the big 'C' had been unkind to both women, but in different ways.

The upstairs door opened, and someone navigated the stairs. Glancing up, she saw Master Ian enter the lounge. The men rarely came into the ladies' locker room, but it didn't faze anyone when they did. It wasn't as if they hadn't seen most of the women naked at one time or another.

Unable to read Ian's expression, she leaped off Marco's lap and clutched the owner's arm. Her heart jumped to her throat, and she was suddenly afraid for Parker. "Master Ian! Please don't discipline Master Parker. It wasn't his fault. I don't want him to get into trouble. Please don't kick him out of the club. It's all my fault. I should've walked away sooner."

Hysteria bubbled up within her. She was so worried about Parker. Even though the creep was his brother, he wasn't responsible for the man's actions. Marco and Mistress China both growled at her as Ian grabbed her by the shoulders and guided her to an empty chair. "Calm down, Shelby, and sit."

His orders were given in a commanding tone that instantly demanded a response. As an experienced sub, it had the desired effect on her as she let his deep voice rumble through her. She took a deep breath as he continued. "Master Parker knows he broke the rules, and there are consequences for what happened. None of which were your fault, and I don't want to hear those words out of your mouth again. Understand?"

Shit. Didn't they see this wasn't Parker's fault? She didn't want him to be kicked out of The Covenant because of her. Unable to stop the tears from falling down her cheeks, she tried to beg him to understand. "Yes, Sir. But..."

"No buts, Shelby." He squeezed her shoulder. "I didn't revoke Master Parker's membership, but he did receive a suspension for his irresponsible actions. He accepted full blame for what happened and agreed with the punishment. Now, he'll be back in a few minutes to take you home, so why don't you grab your things from your locker and change? Okay?"

Still crying softly, she stood and mumbled, "Yes, Sir."

Ian pulled her into his arms and hugged her. "It'll be okay, little one. I promise. I think the best thing you can do is dry your eyes, and when Master Parker comes back, give him some of your sass we all love so much and let him take care of you. I think it'll make you both feel better, hmm?"

She pulled back and gave him a watery smile. "Yes, Sir. Thank you."

Marco took her arm and hugged her as well while placing a kiss on top of her blue-haired head. "Sweetheart, I'm sorry I wasn't there when you needed me."

Nodding her head against his firm chest, she didn't want him to feel bad. "It's okay, Master Marco. You got there as fast as you could."

He gave her another squeeze before letting her go. She trudged into the locker area and found the one she used. Opening it, she pulled off her wig, tossed it into her duffel bag, and ran a hand through her spiked blonde hair. Her cheek still stung, and a quick glance in the mirror showed a bruise had already formed. *Damn.*

Tomorrow and Sunday, she could stay home, but hopefully, some makeup would cover the black and blue so she didn't have to answer twenty questions at work on Monday morning. The four other women she worked with in the human resources department at Tri-Labs Pharmaceuticals would notice it immediately and want to kick someone's ass for hurting her. They were a close group and, for the most part, had each other's backs. Her dickhead boss was another story altogether. He hated when his employees' lives interfered with work for any reason. The prick had gotten pissed off recently when one of the women had a bad asthma attack, and the paramedics had to be called. The way he bitched, you'd think the poor woman had scheduled it just to inconvenience him.

Quickly changing into her sweatpants, T-shirt, and favorite pink, high-top Converse sneakers, she stuffed her mini-skirt into the duffel and then grabbed her purse. At five-foot-four and a size eight, the twenty-nine-year-old was actually looking forward to turning thirty in a few months. Most women might bitch about leaving their twenties behind, but for Shelby, it meant she had survived another year—she was still alive, and that was something to cheer about. However, she was also alone—something which sucked. But she would never get involved with a man, only to have him realize that she wasn't a whole woman and couldn't give him children.

Closing the locker, she picked up her bags and returned to the sitting area. Master Ian was crouched in front of Angie, who appeared worried about something, but it wasn't Shelby's place to interfere with a

Dom and sub. Ian stood and handed her the icepack again as the door to the stairs opened, and Parker walked in, his brown eyes finding her immediately. There was still worry and regret in them, and Shelby felt bad she had ruined everyone's evening.

But damn, the man was gorgeous. He was almost six feet tall, and while he wasn't as cut as Marco or Brody, he had the body of a man used to manual labor. His blond crewcut was receding a little, but it didn't bother her—she still thought he was a dreamboat. Unfortunately, he just wasn't her dreamboat.

Parker hurried over to her and took her duffel from her. "Come on, sweetheart. I'll take you home. Tiny is having one of the guards follow us in your car."

"But, I can—"

"Not negotiable, Shelby." When she reluctantly nodded, he put his arm around her, tucked her into his side, and turned toward Ian. "I'll call you tomorrow about the schedule."

As Ian dipped his head in acknowledgment, Parker led her to the stairs, up to the lobby, and out into the parking lot. The temperature had dropped to a cool fifty-two degrees, and Shelby regretted not bringing her sweatshirt when a shiver went through her. The Dom pulled her tighter against him, and she almost sighed at his warmth. Her car was parked near his truck, and two guards were waiting for them.

Parker came to a stop. "Give Kent your keys, sweetheart. Anthony will follow us, too, and give him a ride back."

After handing over her keys, she let Parker help her into his truck. He pulled the seatbelt across her lap and clicked it in place. Shelby thought it was sweet that he was so attentive to her even though she could've done it herself.

He's a Dom, ding-dong. He would do this for any submissive. Stop mooning over him and get a grip. He deserves someone who can make his life complete, and that's not you.

Sighing, she settled in for the ride home.

CHAPTER THREE

Three Months Later...

"Goddamn it." Sighing, Parker sat back in his office chair and flexed his cramped hand. The one thing he hated about his business was the amount of paperwork required for building permits, purchases, and construction bids. And Thursdays were the worst because he had to sign all the paychecks so they could be distributed the next day. He'd rather be out with his workers, pounding nails over at the construction site of a new strip mall. Instead, he was here, reviewing and signing a massive stack of papers his secretary had prepared for him, and after an hour, he was only halfway done.

New Horizons had seen another company growth spurt recently, and it was time he started thinking about expanding the office and maybe bringing in a partner. One of his college buddies was going through a divorce, and since there were no kids involved, he was thinking of relocating to the Tampa area. Parker made a mental note to call the guy in the next few days and see what he thought about coming aboard. The first thing he was going to do, though, was contract a payroll company because, on Thursdays, it sucked to be him.

Opening and closing his fist, he shut his eyes for a second and thought back to last Sunday night at the club. It'd been his final shift on suspension, and he'd been the DM stationed near the spanking benches of all places. Everything had been going well until Master Carter led Shelby over for a scene within ten feet of Parker. Her color for the night had been purple, with her wig, bra, and polka-dot miniskirt all matching as usual. Damn, she'd looked so cute and so delicious. And she'd avoided eye contact with him, just like she'd been doing for the past twelve weeks. Twelve *long* weeks.

Every night, it had been getting harder and harder to see Shelby scening with other Doms. Yes, she was selective, but he still couldn't figure out why he was one of the men she turned down. There had been times when they'd talked at the bar, usually with a few other people, and it'd appeared they got along. But ever since the night his brother had hit her, she'd been evading him. He didn't blame her for being mad, but he'd tried to apologize many times, starting with when he'd driven her home.

Pulling into the parking lot of Shelby's condo complex, Parker was pleased to see she lived in a nice, safe neighborhood. Aside from giving him directions, she'd remained quiet during the ten-minute drive, and he found himself wanting to know more about her life outside of the club. Where did she work? Did she have family in the area? What did she like to do for fun when she wasn't at the club?

As soon as he put the SUV in park, Shelby reached for the door handle. "Thanks for dropping me off."

Parker growled. Oh, no. No way was she brushing him off tonight. "If you open that door, I'll throw you over my knee and spank your ass until you can't sit. And if you think I'm dropping you off in the parking lot, you better think again, Shelby. I brought you home so I could take care of you, and this is the last time I will say it—this is not negotiable. Now stay there until I come around and open the door for you."

Satisfied when her jaw, gaze, and hand all dropped, he climbed out of the truck and walked around the trunk. Kent had already parked her car and tossed him the keys before getting into the other guard's vehicle and driving away. Pocketing the set, Parker opened the passenger door and held out his hand for Shelby to take. When was the last time she'd been with a Dom, or any man for that matter, outside of the club? One who treated her like the lady she was and opened doors for her or pulled out a chair so she could sit.

The questions flew from his mind when she placed her hand in his and stood. Her skin was soft and smooth, and when she let go of him, he had to make a fist to keep from snatching her hand back. Half a step behind her and carrying her duffel, he followed her to her unit, took out her keys, and opened the door. She hesitated a moment before walking in, and he wondered if she was worried about being alone with him. He prayed she at least knew him well enough to know he wasn't anything like his brother, who he'd literally dropped inside the asshole's motel room door. The now conscious but groggy bastard could either crawl to the bed or sleep on the floor—it didn't matter to Parker. Dave was lucky he hadn't been beaten into a coma.

Parker dropped her bag next to the foyer closet, not knowing where Shelby wanted it, and trailed her into the little eat-in kitchen. Walking straight to her refrigerator, he opened the freezer and found an ice pack. After wrapping it in a towel he removed from the handle of her oven, he gave it to her. "Put that on your cheek for a bit. Do you have any alcohol—wine or something? Something to stop your shivering."

"Irish whiskey. Bottom shelf of the pantry."

He raised an eyebrow but didn't argue her choice since he could use a shot himself. Locating the bottle in the pantry next to the fridge, he looked at her questioningly, and she pointed to an upper cabinet next to the sink. Grabbing two rocks glasses, he filled them a third of the way up, then returned the bottle to its perch. Taking the glasses, he turned toward Shelby. "Go sit in your living room and get comfortable. I'm only staying a little while until I know you're okay."

What he didn't add was that he hoped she wouldn't want him to leave. Again, she hesitated, but he waited patiently. He was determined for her to see the caring, gentle side of him, and maybe he could find out what she had against him. When she finally led the way into her living area, he followed and handed her one of the glasses after she sat on the sofa. There were two recliners and a loveseat, but he chose the other end of the couch. Close enough to inhale her strawberry-scented shampoo but far enough away that he wasn't crowding her.

"You don't have to stay, Parker. I'm fine."

"Why don't you like me?" Okay, that's not what he expected to blurt out of his mouth, but there it was. From her wide-eyed expression, she hadn't anticipated it either. "I mean, what have I done that makes you avoid me?"

"I... I don't know what you're talking about."

Parker rolled his eyes. "Don't give me that, Shelby. I'm not stupid. I've asked you twice to play at the club, and both times, you turned me down, so I stopped asking. It's obvious you want nothing to do with me, so tell me why. I'm a big boy—I can take it. Is it my personality? My looks? Do I have bad breath? What?"

She licked her lips, and his eyes zeroed in on the movement. Shaking her head, she stood, left her drink on the coffee table, and began pacing the room. "It's none of those things. I mean, it's not you—it's me."

"Bullshit. I hate that freaking cliché." He stood,

clunking his untouched drink on the table next to hers. "But I guess if that's all you've got, then there's no point in me sticking around. I'm sorry about what happened with Dave. You'll never know how sorry I am."

He let out a heavy breath. He knew he should leave, but there was one thing he had to do first. Stepping toward her, Parker gently cupped her bruised cheek. Not waiting for a response, he leaned down and kissed her. Flat out kissed her. If this were his only chance, he'd take it. For a brief moment, she melted into him, and his heart leaped for joy, along with his cock, but then she stiffened, and he knew he'd lost her. Hell, he'd never even had her.

Releasing her, he gazed at her with all his regret and frustration.

"Goodbye, Shelby."

Damn. Why couldn't he get past that night? Get past that kiss? He'd jacked off to that kiss more times than he wanted to count. Watching Carter spank her, plug her ass, and finger fuck her to several orgasms last night had driven him fucking bonkers. It was all he could do to keep an eye on the other scenes to make sure no submissives were in danger of being harmed. What he'd really wanted to do was punch the living daylights out of the other Dom and never let another man touch his sweet Shelby.

She's not yours, you dumb fuck. And she never will be.

His cell phone rang, and he groaned when he saw the name on its screen. "Hello, Mother."

"Parker, it's so nice to hear your voice. How are you, darling?"

Pulling the phone away from his ear, he stared at it in confusion momentarily. Parker's relationship with his mother was almost as bad as that with his father. Phone calls were rare, and they were never just for niceties. There had to be a reason other than calling to say hello as ordinary people did. He snorted—his family was far from ordinary. "I'm fine, Mother, and you?"

"Wonderful, dear. I was wondering when you were planning on coming up for a visit. It would be a pleasure to see you again. I ran into Cynthia Holloway yesterday. She's moved back to Boston and hoped to see you and catch up on old times."

All right. A picture was beginning to form, but for the life of him, he couldn't figure out what it was. He and Cynthia had gone to a private high school together, and her parents and his were good friends. They'd also been friends who'd gone their separate ways after graduation despite their parents' insistence that they become a couple. She was pretty and sweet, but there had never been a spark between them. He hadn't seen her since his brother's wedding five years ago, when they had briefly caught up with each other's lives.

"I'm not sure when I can get away, Mother. It's a busy time for me."

"Too busy to come visit your family? I'm sure your little company can survive without you for a few days."

He could hear the false pout and condescension in her voice, and it made him cringe. Damn. Was his family phony and snobby or what? "Actually, Mother, business is booming. So, yes, I am too busy to visit at the moment. As a matter of fact, I have to take another call. Tell Cynthia I said hello."

Not waiting for a response, he disconnected the call. Rubbing his index finger over his bottom lip, he wondered what the call had really been about. His brother had called five times in the last three days, but as soon as Parker heard the first few words of the voicemails to make sure no one was dead or injured, he'd erased them.

A snore came from the floor beside him, and he glanced down at his one-hundred-twenty-pound Bullmastiff. That dog could sleep through a bomb going off. He lay on his back with all four paws twitching in the air as if he were chasing a dream squirrel—the big goofball. On days like this, the human was jealous of the canine, who led such a simple, carefree life, now that he'd been rescued by someone who loved him. Aggravated that he wanted to trade places with an animal that drank out of a toilet, Parker did the only thing he could think of to get

Shelby and his fucked-up family off his mind—he attacked the remaining stack of paperwork.

Damn. It's going to be a long day.

Shelby stared at her image in the mirror and turned to see the dress from every angle. Kristen Anders, soon-to-be-Sawyer, had picked out the most flattering bridesmaid dresses she'd ever seen. The navy, silk, one-shoulder dress stopped right above the knee and could easily be worn again for another occasion—unlike the dress Shelby still had stuffed in the back of her closet from her cousin's wedding three years ago. That Pepto-Bismol pink, ruffled satin and taffeta monstrosity had been hideous, especially when paired with the matching parasol she'd had to carry. A shudder went down her spine at the memory.

"Shelby, you look fantastic in that dress," Kristen squealed from her seat in the bridal shop showroom. "I'm so glad we all agreed on it because it's perfect for everyone. And I don't think you'll need as much altering as the others."

Angie Beckett, who was now engaged to Kristen's future brother-in-law, and their friend, Kayla London, were being attended to by two seamstresses who were pinning their dresses in all the right places. The fourth and final bridesmaid, Jenn Mullins, the Sawyer brothers' niece, had just gingerly changed out of her own dress, trying not to stick herself with all the pins that'd been needed. It was a little over two months before the wedding, and the girls had decided to go out to lunch after the fittings.

Shelby turned around to face Kristen. "I love it, and I'm so glad you went with the navy instead of black, which is so played out these days. Did Will get his tuxedo picked out yet?"

Will Anders, Kristen's cousin, would be her man of honor since he'd been her closest friend and relative after her divorce from her cheating first husband. Will had influenced her to move to Tampa after the split, leading her to meet and fall in love with Devon.

Kristen nodded. "Yup. We went the other day and decided to go with a white tux since the rest of the Sexy Six-Pack and Dev's brother, Nick, will all be in their Navy dress whites."

The women laughed at Kristen's nickname for the six former Navy SEALs who made up the Trident Security team. In addition to her fiancé, Devon, and his eldest brother, Ian, the rest of the hunky men were Marco, Brody, Ben Michaelson—also known as Boomer—and Jake Donovan.

"It's one of the reasons I went with a blush-colored dress. That and it's my second, and last, mind you, wedding. I swear I'm never going through this again. It's way too stressful."

Shelby gave her a half-hearted smile. What she

wouldn't give for things to be different, and she could experience the stress of planning her own wedding. Instead, she was stressed out about the test results, which would be in tomorrow. Last week, while showering, she'd found a lump under her left arm and immediately scheduled a biopsy with her oncologist. Most people would have assumed it was an ingrown hair or would have waited a few weeks to see if it disappeared. But after going through cancer once before, Shelby was well aware of the different signs and symptoms to look out for.

She dreaded the word she knew in her heart that her doctor would say—lymphoma. Hopefully, she'd caught it early again, and it would be treatable. Out of all the cancers out there, the statistics for remission were highest for cancer of the lymph nodes. Well, she beat the big "C" before, and she could beat it again. For now, she would try to enjoy the girls' day out.

"I think the blush color is perfect for you." When the seamstress told her she was ready to pin her up, Shelby stepped over to the riser Angie had come down from moments before. "And the dress is stunning. Devon is going to drool when he sees you."

Jenn giggled as she sat next to Kristen. "Uncle Devon drools every time he sees her."

"This is true."

"So, what about you, Shelby?" Jenn asked. "I know you've never been married, but did you ever come close?"

Keeping the rest of her body still for the seam-stress, she shook her head. "Nope. And I don't think I'll ever get married."

Kayla stepped off her riser. "Why not? Girl, you've got Doms tripping over themselves to get to you. Especially Parker."

Parker. Just hearing his name made her wet and had her thinking back to that one kiss they'd shared. For a brief moment, she'd surrendered to him. Sometime in the past few months, she stopped trying to kid herself that she'd melted because he'd caught her off-guard. The real reason was the electricity that had shot from her lips to her pussy.

Damn, that man could kiss. Hot. Wet. Demanding. She'd been about to give in and beg him to take her to bed until she remembered all the reasons why it was a bad idea. Then, she'd cried herself to sleep after he'd walked out the door—and had avoided him ever since. With a very good possibility of her cancer coming back, she was convinced she'd made the right decision.

She shrugged her shoulders. "He's nice, but I'm not looking for anything permanent. I like being single." Shit. Even she didn't believe that lie as she noticed the other women glancing at each other. Better nip it in the bud before they start their match-making. "Besides, we aren't compatible. Yummy Carter is more my type, and he'll never settle down. I still can't believe he killed those men who kidnapped

Kat the other day and shot Boomer's dad. Boomer must be so relieved she's okay and that his father will make it too."

Kat was the Dom's high school girlfriend, who he thought had died years ago. But as fate would have it, she'd been in the Witness Protection Program with her father because Russian mobsters were after him and had murdered his wife and son. Kat recently resurfaced and ran to Boomer for help when she realized someone was stalking her after her father died for real a few months earlier.

"Well, he's relieved Rick is going to be okay and is being released over the weekend, but Boomer's freaked out because Kat took off on him. We don't know what went wrong with them, but I hope it works out. I think they are perfect for one another." Kristen snorted. "Oh, and I wouldn't be too sure of Carter not settling down. I think there's a woman out there who will put that man in his place. Until then, the rest of us get to enjoy him—well, some of us do, since Kayla doesn't do guys, Angie and Ian don't share, and Jenn thinks of him as another uncle."

Turning around for the seamstress, Shelby sighed in relief when the others switched the conversation to where they should go for lunch. The last thing she needed was them figuring out she secretly longed to be Parker Christiansen's submissive and, yes, his wife. But that would never happen.

CHAPTER FOUR

It had been over two weeks since Parker's suspension was lifted, and he'd yet to play at the club. It wasn't that none of the subs had requested to scene with him, but because he'd turned each one down. He couldn't get Shelby out of his mind, especially since he hadn't seen her since the night she'd played with Carter—the prick—the last night of Parker's suspension.

Damn. He had to get his emotions under control. The other Dom hadn't done anything wrong, but he was the last one Parker had watched bring Shelby to an orgasm. Carter was a nice guy. However, from what Parker understood, the man could kill him without blinking an eye. Not the type of person you wanted to piss off.

If Shelby wasn't there again tonight, Parker would drive to her place to find out where she was. Had she stopped coming because he was free to play again, and she didn't want him to try negotiating with her again? He didn't think that was the reason. She'd been firm in the past when she'd turned him down. But tonight, he would find out what she had against him, and then he'd fix it because he was beyond obsessed with her.

Every time he licked his lips, he remembered how she'd tasted. For that brief moment, she'd given in to him, and he was confident that if he chipped away at her resolve, he could win her over. Something was holding her back from becoming exclusive to him or any other Dom, and he was determined to find out what it was.

After two complete trips around the club, which included asking most of the subs and a few of the Doms if they'd seen her, he knew he had to change tactics. No one seemed to know where she was or why she hadn't been there. Glancing around, he didn't see Ian or Devon anywhere, so he made a beeline to Mitch, chatting with a few members at the bar.

When there was a break in the conversation, he clapped the manager on the shoulder. "Can I talk to you in your office for a minute?"

Mitch nodded. It wasn't unusual for the man to receive requests for a private conversation. "Sure." He addressed the group he'd been speaking with. "If you'll excuse me... I'll be back in a few."

Parker followed him toward the opposite end of the second floor. On this side, there was also a fetish shop stocked with sex toys, wigs, lingerie, and anything else the members were interested in purchasing. They took the hallway to the right of the shop, which led to the offices and stock room. Mitch unlocked his office door with a scan of his palm print. It was how all the doors and gates at the compound were opened. The system could also allow a person only to have access to certain places. Parker knew this from working on the interior construction of all the buildings.

Shutting the door behind them, Parker took a seat on the near side of the desk as Mitch sat in his chair behind it. He didn't bother with pleasantries. "Where's Shelby been?"

Mitch raised an eyebrow at him, then sat back in the chair. "Why do you think I know where she is?"

"Don't fuck with me, Mitch, I'm not in the mood. You and Ian know everything about everybody here… especially the subs. If one of them suddenly stopped coming, you would either know why in advance or you'd be pounding on their door to find out what was wrong. Now, what's going on with Shelby? She hasn't been here in two weeks."

The other man sighed. "I'm not at liberty to discuss it with you, Park. I'm sorry. But I didn't know you were interested in her since I've never seen you play together."

"Well, it's not from lack of trying on my part," he ground out. "Damn it, can you at least give me a hint here? Did she sign a contract with anyone? Is she still a fucking member?"

Tilting his head to the side, Mitch considered him for a moment. Parker wanted to reach across the desk and shake the information out of the guy, but that would definitely get him tossed from the club, so he waited.

Almost a full minute went by before Mitch seemed to make up his mind. "She's still a member and didn't sign a contract with anyone that I'm aware of. All I can say is she took some time off from the club for personal reasons."

There was more to it, Parker was convinced. The owners were highly protective of the club's submissives and knew almost everything about them, which was why he'd come to Mitch in the first place.

"Didn't you drive her home the night that your dick-head brother was here?"

"Yeah." His blood neared the boiling point again, as it always did when he remembered how Dave had hit Shelby. He hadn't spoken to the bastard since, although his brother had left numerous messages on his voicemail, trying to apologize. Parker wasn't accepting any part of it.

"Well, what are you doing sitting here in my office then?"

He got it. Mitch wouldn't break a member's trust, but nothing would stop Parker from going to her condo and pounding on her door. When he stood,

Mitch stopped him with his hand up. "But one thing, Park. Take it easy with her, okay?"

His brows furrowed. "What do you mean?"

"If she doesn't want to tell you, then back off. I mean it. If I find out you went there high-handed, we'll have a problem, you and me. I think she needs a caring Dom at the moment, not an overbearing one. That's all I'm going to say."

Parker was confused. What the hell was wrong with her? Knowing he wasn't getting any more information, he nodded and then hurried out of the office. Tonight, he was going to find out what was going on with her, and then he'd fix it before telling her he had every intention of making her his. It was time Ms. Shelby Whitman had a full-time Dom... and it was going to be him.

After flushing the toilet, Shelby reached for the mouthwash. Her stomach was reacting violently to the second round of chemo, and she was having trouble keeping food down. Someone from the pharmacy should be there soon, bringing her new prescription for anti-nausea pills. She'd forgotten to pick them up after leaving the treatment center two days ago and regretted it since late this afternoon. The first round of chemo hadn't affected her this way, but she was told to expect a cumulative effect as her treatments went on. Thankfully, the pharmacy was open late tonight, and they had a delivery service.

Staring at her reflection in the mirror, she winced. Hopefully, she'd get a good night's sleep tonight and look better in the morning. If anyone saw her now, they'd think she had the flu or something. Although someone with the flu probably looked better than this —red eyes, pale face, hair sticking out in all directions, and wearing her favorite flannel pajamas because she was so cold. Thinking back, this was worse than when she'd received radiation following the removal of her ovaries and the hysterectomy six and a half years ago. At least, she thought it was.

As she shuffled out to the living room couch, the doorbell rang. Hoping it was her prescription, she hurried to the door and opened it without checking to see who it was. *Damn.* She should have peeked through the peephole first. "Parker? W-what are you doing here?"

The man raised an eyebrow and crossed his arms. *Oh, shit.* He was in full Dom mode, complete with his club leathers and boots. The snug T-shirt emphasized his strong shoulders and chest. From the expression on his face, it was apparent something was wrong.

"Checking on you. And from the look of things, I'm glad I did. Why haven't you been to the club lately? You've been sick this whole time?"

Shelby tried to downplay her illness. "It's just the flu. I'll be fine in a few days."

His frown said he didn't believe her. "The flu doesn't last two weeks, Shelby."

"Well, I had some other stuff I was taking care of last week. I'll be back soon. Thanks for stopping by." When she started to shut the door, he stuck his foot out, preventing her from closing it all the way. Movement over his shoulder caught her attention, and she realized the driver from the pharmacy had arrived.

"Ms. Whitman?"

She sighed as Parker turned to face the college-age deliveryman. "Yes, I'm Shelby Whitman. Thanks for bringing it over."

"No problem." He handed her a clipboard. "Sign here, please. And Mr. Carlson said to tell you he sent over a bag of ginger candies and some ginger tea—no charge. He said that a lot of his patients on chemo find they help with the nausea when combined with the medicine."

Shelby winced when Parker's jaw dropped, eyes popped, and fists clenched. *Shit.* Signing the form, she handed it back to the driver, who clearly didn't realize he'd dropped a bomb between the other two people. "Thanks. Wait a second, please."

She was about to grab her purse for a tip, but Parker's growl stopped her. He pulled out his wallet, handed the kid a twenty, and then took the pharmacy bag. "Thanks. I'll make sure Ms. Whitman uses all of it."

Happy about the big tip, the driver waved as he jogged to his car. "No problem. If you need anything else, give us a call."

Shelby tried to take the bag from Parker, but the frown on the Dom's face had her backing up into the foyer. Fuck, she was in so much trouble.

Chemo? She was suffering the effects of chemotherapy and tried to tell him it was the flu? This couldn't be happening. His gut churned as the realization sunk in —his sweet Shelby had cancer. And Mitch had known. This was what he'd been talking about. Or did the club owners truly know what was going on?

Parker couldn't imagine any of the Doms from The Covenant allowing her to go through this alone. But Mitch had been right about one thing—Shelby needed a gentle Dom right now, not an arrogant one. When she stepped backward, away from him, he realized he was scaring her. He tried to relax the tension coursing through him and followed her inside, closing the door behind him.

Now that he knew what was wrong, he could properly care for her. First things first. He brushed past her, entered the kitchen, and promptly grabbed her tea kettle from the stove, filling it with water. Opening the cabinet where he remembered her glasses were kept, he found a coffee mug. He then pulled the medication bottle from the bag and read the label. All the while, he knew Shelby was silently standing in the doorway watching him. "It says to take one pill first, and if you need to, you can take another one."

He filled a glass with water, handed it to her along with a pill, and watched as she dutifully took the medication. Her pale face and sunken eyes worried him. "Go lie down. I can tell you're exhausted. I'll bring the tea when it's ready."

"You don't have to do this. I can take care of myself."

Taking the glass from her, he turned toward the sink. "Not negotiable, Shelby. Now, unless you want to start racking up some punishments for when you're feeling better, I suggest you follow orders. Go lie down."

She glared at him for a moment, but he wasn't backing down. Shelby needed someone to take care of her, and whether she realized it yet or not, he'd just signed up for the job. Finally, she heeded his command.

He didn't like how sick she looked. After he got some information from her, he'd retrieve his laptop from the truck and do some research while she slept.

When the boiling water was ready, he poured it into the mug and steeped the teabag. Opening her pantry, he found a honey jar and added a drop. Growing up, it was how his nanny enjoyed it, and since Shelby had honey in the house, it was a good bet she used it in her tea. After draining the little bag and tossing it into the garbage under the sink, he found a spoon in one of the drawers and stirred the heated drink. On his way out to the living room, where he'd heard her turn on the TV, he grabbed the small bag of ginger candies.

Shelby was sitting on the couch watching the news, and he frowned at her. "You're supposed to be lying down, sweetheart."

"I can't drink the tea if I'm lying down, *Sir*."

He paused at her snarky use of the title. Raising an eyebrow, he handed her the tea. "Drink up, brat. And where can I find a blanket for you? I want you comfortable while we talk." He held up a hand when it appeared she would argue with him. "Not negotiable."

Letting out a heavy sigh, she pointed to the hallway behind him. "You like those two words way too much. In the linen closet next to the bathroom, bottom shelf."

Nodding, he turned and retrieved a heavy, knitted afghan. While she drank her tea, he wrapped the blanket around her, returned to the kitchen, and found her bottle of Irish whiskey. He was going to need a drink for this conversation. The only thing he could figure out so far was that if she was receiving chemo, the cancer wasn't considered terminal... yet. And he prayed it never reached that point. The world would be much darker if Ms. Shelby Whitman weren't in it.

When he walked back into the living room, she placed the almost empty cup on the coffee table and swung her legs up on the couch. He grabbed a second throw pillow and tucked it with the one under her head. "Comfy?"

"Yes, thank you. I'm sorry I was so bitchy before. I've been throwing up all evening, and I'm tired and achy."

He sat in the recliner facing her and sipped his whiskey. "I understand that. What I don't understand is why you kept this a secret and why no one is here helping you."

Shimmying down further, she turned to lay on her side. Her eyes were getting heavy. "I didn't want to worry everyone. As for someone helping me, I don't want to be a burden to anyone. My parents have been gone for several years, and my only sister lives in Michigan with her own family. I didn't want any of my friends to feel obligated to help, so I kept it to myself. I've gone through this before, so I know what to expect and what to do."

"What?" He gaped at her in shock. "You've had cancer before? When?"

"Almost seven years ago. I went through radiation that time, though. No chemo. I've been in remission for six years. A little over two weeks ago, I found a lump under my arm and called my oncologist right away. The biopsy and other tests revealed lymphoma. Non-Hodgkin's. Stage one. I started chemo last week, and this was my second round."

His shock turned to anger, but he tried to keep it from showing. There was no way she was going through this alone. Mentally, he formulated a plan and knew it wasn't one she was going to be happy with, but, fuck that, he wasn't giving her a choice.

Opening his mouth, he quickly closed it again and stared at her. She must have been exhausted because she had fallen asleep within seconds of closing her eyes.

Yup. Shelby had a new Dom in her life, and if Parker had anything to say about it, it would be permanent.

CHAPTER FIVE

S helby woke to the smell of coffee and was grateful her nausea was minimal this morning. *Wait a minute... coffee?*

It was then she remembered Parker. He must have stayed all night because it was a little after seven, and somehow, she'd ended up in her bed. Stretching, she glanced around, and confusion struck her. Neatly lined up next to her closet were her two suitcases and several duffel bags... and from their appearance, they were full.

What the hell is he up to?

Well, first, she had to take care of her bladder. Climbing out of bed and shuffling to the bathroom, she took care of the necessities of life. Why had he stayed? She hated to admit it, but it was nice knowing he had, even after she'd been rude to him and then fallen asleep less than five minutes after getting comfortable on the couch.

After flushing and washing her hands and face, she brushed her teeth and then headed out to the kitchen. Sitting at her dinette table, Parker's back was to her, and she took a moment to study him. He was typing away on his laptop and talking softly on his cell. From the sound of it, it was construction business related. He must not have heard her get up and was trying to be quiet and not wake her.

He was no longer in his leather pants and boots but instead a pair of sweats, a new T-shirt, and sneakers. Either he'd left and returned, or he kept a spare set of clothes in his truck. If she were to guess, it was the latter. A cup of coffee sat next to his laptop. What would it be like to wake up to this domestic scene every morning?

"Hey, didn't hear you come in. Are you hungry?"

She'd been lost in her daydream and hadn't noticed him hang up his phone. "Um... a little. I'll just make some toast. That should stay down."

He stood and held out the chair next to him. "Sit. I'll get it. Butter or jelly?"

Stunned, she watched him take over her kitchen like he'd lived there for years, pulling out her bread and popping two pieces in her toaster. A warm, fuzzy feeling came over her as she took the seat. "Um... a little butter and some honey, please."

A smile spread across his face. "Butter and honey it

is. Something to drink? I'm not sure if coffee would sit well in your stomach."

"Milk, please."

After he placed the full glass in front of her and turned to attend to her toast, she bit her bottom lip. "Is there a reason why my suitcases and duffels are out?"

"Yup. You're coming to stay at my place while you go through your treatments."

Shelby's mouth dropped open. He couldn't be serious. But when he brought her toast over, she could see by his expression that he was very serious. "I—I can't do that. I mean, you have your business and everything."

He pulled out his chair and rotated it before straddling the seat. "You can do it, and you will. As for my business... I'm the boss. Every once in a while, I'll need to run out and check on things, but I can do a lot of things from home with my computer and phone. That's why I have foremen working for me."

His voice softened. "You need someone to watch over you, Shelby. And that someone is going to be me." He smirked. "Not negotiable. I've even drawn up a contract between us."

She took the piece of paper he picked up and handed her, scanning it in shock. Holy crap, he was very, very serious.

"I used the basic contract from the club. Essentially, it says that I'll be in charge of your physical, emotional, and mental well-being while you undergo your chemo. All I expect in return is your obedience and a promise you'll do everything in your power to kick this cancer's ass. I even added a no-sexual contact clause at the bottom, so you don't have to worry about me hitting on you. Then again, that would make me an ass for propositioning a woman in your current condition."

Her eyes filled with tears. It'd been so long since she'd had someone to lean on. Her parents had come the last time she was ill, but they were both gone now. She cleared the lump in her throat and shook her head. "I can't ask you to do this, Parker."

"I don't recall wanting you to ask me. You need someone to care for you, and I can do it. Now, I've been doing a lot of research on Non-Hodgkin's, and I have a bunch of questions for your doctor. I got his name from your prescription bottle and made an appointment for us to see him tomorrow. I see from the schedule you posted on the fridge that your next treatment is on Monday—I'll be taking you to it. What about your job? Can you take a leave of absence? I don't want you working during this. Hell, I don't even know what you do for a living. I mean..."

He was on a roll, and she had to stop him. "Parker, wait... this—this is all too much. I can't move in with you. Do you realize I'll be getting chemo for the next six weeks at least? I work in the human resources department at Tri-Labs. My boss is pissed-off enough already that I need six Mondays off in a row. I had to leave early yesterday and took off today because I was sick. I can't take a leave of absence."

His eyes narrowed. "Why not? By law, they have to give it to you. If you want, I'll talk with your boss and tell him he can either okay the time off or get his ass kicked. And if you're worried about finances, I can cover everything until you're better. There's plenty of room at my house, and because I can be a bit of a slob, I have a housekeeper who comes twice a week. I'll arrange for her to come more often. You won't have to worry about anything but getting better."

Was he crazy? Was she dreaming? "Why?"

"Why what?"

"Why are you doing all of this?"

Parker took her hand and brought it to his lips. "Because I'm a Dom and because I care about you. Isn't that enough?"

God, he hoped it was enough. Those were precisely the reasons why he was doing this. However, the bonus kicker was that he would get to know her better and vice versa. One thing still bothered him, and he had to ask her about it. "Tell me something. Why didn't Mitch or Ian step forward to help you? I know damn well neither one of them would have left you to suffer through this alone. What did you tell them?"

Shelby shrugged and bit her bottom lip. "I kind of downplayed it. I told them I had some personal family issues going on and needed to suspend my membership for a few weeks. They wanted to help, but I told them I'd be okay. Trust me, they tried very hard to find out what was going on, but again, I didn't want anyone to feel obligated to help."

Shaking his head, Parker growled. "You've been in the lifestyle for years, Shelby. You know damn well we're a close-knit community. Nobody says they want to help because they feel obligated to. They say it because they care and know if the situation were reversed, you'd be there for them. They love you, baby. You're family to everyone at The Covenant. Why don't you see that?"

Her eyes filled with tears, and he stood before her, drawing her into his arms. He hadn't intended to make her cry, but she needed to hear she wasn't alone in this fight. When she took a shuddering breath, he held her tighter. "Let me tell a few people—you'll need help whether you realize it or not. I'm moving you in with me, but in case I need to tend to business, I want to be able to call someone to stay with you."

She pulled away to glare at him. "I don't need a babysitter, Parker. I'm a grown woman."

"I didn't say you needed a babysitter. I said you needed your friends and family. They would feel slighted if you didn't turn to them when you needed them the most." He let her go and handed her a napkin to wipe her eyes and nose.

"You're going to say this is not negotiable, aren't you?"

She blew her nose, and he couldn't help but think even that was adorable when she did it. "Yes, I am. And whether you admit it or not, it's what you want me to say. Now, eat, and then see if you need anything else I didn't pack. I put in your clothes, underwear, toiletries, pajamas, medications, and anything else I could think of. I also grabbed your cell phone charger and your e-reader."

"Wow. You thought of everything, didn't you?"

He winked at her as he shut down his laptop and put it back into its carrying bag. "I hope so, but just in case, you better look. I'll come back later with a cooler and empty your fridge so nothing spoils. Oh, you're not allergic to or afraid of dogs, are you?"

"No, why? Do you have one?"

Grabbing his now-cold coffee, he dumped it into the sink and cleaned the mug. "Yeah. I've always loved animals but wasn't allowed them growing up. My parents were not animal lovers—hell, they're not even children lovers. Anyway, I called my neighbor and asked him to let Spanky out last night and this morning.

Shelby choked on her milk. "Spanky? You have a dog named Spanky?"

A chuckle escaped him, along with an impish grin. Putting one hand over his heart, he held up his other. "I swear, it's the name they gave him at the animal rescue. It was too ironic to change."

The lyrical laugh that came from her mouth filled his heart. It was nice to have her bubbly personality showing once again. Two weeks was way too long not to see her smile and watch her eyes light up in amusement. He vowed then and there to make her laugh as often as possible—for as long as she let him.

CHAPTER SIX

"This is your house? It's beautiful." Shelby couldn't help the awe in her voice. The one-level ranch house was gorgeous, with stunning landscaping surrounding it. The neighborhood was quiet at the moment, but she could tell many young families lived there because of the jungle gyms in some of the backyards, along with the bicycles and toys in a few driveways. They'd passed an elementary school and park two blocks away, making it an ideal area for raising children. She pushed the thought from her mind.

"Yup. One of the perks of being a builder. This was a foreclosure and was in desperate need of repair when I bought it. The neighbors were thrilled when I renovated it." Parker pulled up to the two-car garage and killed the engine. "Stay there, I'll get your door."

She sighed and waited. He wasn't exactly treating her as an invalid because common courtesies, like opening doors and pulling out chairs, were something most Doms did for any submissive. But part of her wished she wasn't just any submissive to him.

Stop it. That kind of thinking will only cause heartache for you both.

Her door opened, and she took his outstretched hand, letting him help her out of the truck. He gestured for her to lead the way to the front door. "I'll come back out for your things once I have you settled."

When he unlocked and pushed on the front door, they were immediately met by a giant, brown Bullmastiff, wagging his tail furiously and woofing loudly. The dog sniffed her, then his master, and back to her again before pushing past them to pee on a bush. In a flash, he was beside her again before Parker could shut the door. The dog bounced on all four paws and spun in circles around her.

"Spanky, down boy. Let the poor woman get past the foyer, will you."

Shelby giggled and scratched the dog's head, which was the size of a basketball. "Such a good boy. That's okay. You can ask for some loving any time."

Spanky gave his owner a grin that could only be interpreted as, "See? She likes me, so shut up."

Parker nudged the massive fur ball with his leg until they had room to pass. "Go get a treat."

The dog bounded toward the kitchen and, moments later, met them in the living room, carrying a covered, hard plastic jar by its handle. He dropped it next to Parker's feet, then waited impatiently for his master to open it and hand over an extra-large dog biscuit. With a full mouth, Spanky took his prize to the corner of the room and plopped down to eat it.

"That's so cute," Shelby gushed. "I think I love him already. He looks a little like the dog, Hooch, from that movie."

Taking her hand, Parker led her into the kitchen. "I know. I love that movie and always wanted a dog like that. He's not exactly the same breed, but similar. I found this woman, Tori, who's involved with a group called Bullmastiff Rescuers, Inc., and she hooked me up with Spanky. He's super smart and a great companion. Most days, I take him to the office and occasionally to job sites, but he can stay here and keep you company if I need to go anywhere. He loves to cuddle and sometimes forgets he's not a lapdog."

"I'd love the company. Thanks." She sat at the dinette set as fatigue started to roll over her again. "I grew up with dogs, but with working full-time, I would feel bad if I left one at home all the time."

"Well, Spanky will love hanging out with you. And if I have to go out, you don't have to walk him. Just open the backdoor, and he'll do his business. I'll pick up after him when I get home."

He handed her the cup of ginger tea he'd prepared

on his Keurig machine. On the way over, her nausea had begun to stir again. "Drink that while I bring in your stuff. The house has four bedrooms, but only one, other than mine, has a bed. The others I use as my office and weight room."

While he went to get her bags, Shelby sipped the tea and glanced around. The house was as beautiful inside as on the outside, but it was obvious a bachelor lived there. No drapes or valances were on the windows, only blinds, and the décor was utilitarian and sparse.

Peeking into what was considered a family room, she noted the large leather sofas and an entertainment center with a sixty-inch TV, stereo, and video game console. The only thing on the side tables were bland, generic lamps. She was sure it worked for him, but it needed a woman's touch. Maybe she could give him some decorating help while she was here—it was the least she could do to thank him for caring for her while she was sick.

The front door opened again, and Parker strode in, carrying all her bags at once. She stood and followed him down the hall and was shocked when he walked into what was clearly his bedroom, placing the bags on the bed. He noticed her stunned expression. "You're sleeping in here because of the attached bath. I'll take the guest room."

"No." She shook her head vehemently. "I can't kick you out of your bedroom. I'll take the guest room…"

Her voice trailed off at the stern expression on his face, and she sighed. "Not negotiable, right?"

"Right." He tilted his head. "You're a little pale. Why don't you go out to the family room and lie down on the sofa while I bring out a pillow and blanket? Then I'll straighten up in here, change the sheets, and move some of my stuff into the other bathroom."

She was quickly learning it was useless to argue with him—after all, he was a Dom and expected to be obeyed. But a benefit of obeying him was she felt pampered and adored. *Damn it.*

After changing the sheets, Parker pulled the comforter up the length of the bed and put the pillow back into place. Spinning around slowly, he inspected the rest of the room. Thank God the housekeeper, Emily, had been there yesterday. She usually changed his bed linens on Mondays, but everything else was neat and clean.

He'd made room in his closet and cleaned out one of the two dressers for Shelby's clothes. The feeling he got seeing her intimates in the top drawer had him wishing they were there permanently.

She's sick, asshole. Now is not the time to be romancing her. Help her get better, and then you can start thinking with your southern head.

He checked the time on his bedside alarm clock. It was a little after one. Shelby needed her afternoon medications soon, which had to be taken with food if possible. Parker would have to go food shopping later to get some of the things she liked to eat, but for now, he could make her a turkey and cheese sandwich.

Glancing into the family room on his way to the kitchen, he saw she was still sleeping on the couch. Spanky was on the floor next to her, his head on his paws, watching over her. The big lug had already put himself on protection duty. Parker knew how he felt—nothing would happen to Shelby if they could help it.

He removed the necessary items from the fridge and made sandwiches for them. Earlier, he'd lined Shelby's medications and nutritional supplements on the counter. Checking each bottle, he took one of each pill that she needed and set them on the plate next to her lunch. Glasses of milk completed the meal, and he carried hers out to the family room before returning for his own.

Squatting next to the sofa, he reached over Spanky to rub Shelby's cheek with the back of his hand. "Baby, I hate to wake you, but you need to take your meds."

Her eyes blinked open, and within seconds, she focused her gaze on him. "Hi. How long was I asleep?"

"About two hours. That chemo must take a lot out of you. I made you a turkey and cheese sandwich but didn't know if you liked mayo or mustard."

Shelby sat up as Spanky did the same next to her.

She scratched his ear, and the dog groaned in delight. "I like both, but I don't think my stomach would accept either right now, so I'll take it plain. Thank you."

Handing her the plate, he pointed at the two glasses on the end table. "I poured you some milk. I figured that was best with the meds."

While he sat on the recliner catty-cornered to her, she nodded. "Thanks. I'll take them after I eat."

He watched as she took a bite of her sandwich and then glanced around the room. Inwardly cringing, he wished he'd gotten around to hiring a decorator. While he could build beautiful houses, when it came to furnishing them, he was all thumbs. Shelby's condo had that homey feel, with her personal touches everywhere. Maybe when she was feeling better, she could help him pick out some pictures, drapes, and stuff.

"So, let's go over a few things."

After swallowing her food, she took a sip of milk. "Okay. Like what?"

"For starters, after we eat, I need you to write a grocery list of foods you like. I'll pack up your fridge and pantry tomorrow, but I can run out later today to get whatever else you like. My research said you need to eat healthy, and I found a bunch of nutritional smoothies with fruits, veggies, and supplements. I can get one of those blender things for you."

She grinned at him. "You don't need to buy one—I have one in the bottom cabinet next to the fridge. I love making them. Although I prefer using it to make margaritas instead."

Chuckling, Parker shook his head. "No alcohol. At least until after your treatments." He laughed harder when Shelby snapped her fingers and pouted. Damn, she was so adorable. "Item number two or three, if you include the no alcohol thing, you'll call your boss and tell him you need to take sick leave. The last thing you need is exhausting yourself more than necessary."

"As much as I hate to say it, you're right. And money isn't an issue—I have some savings, and Mom and Dad left my sister and me a little inheritance. It's not a lot, but more than enough to pay my bills for a while."

He gritted his teeth and didn't argue with her. She wasn't his sub, and he knew she would only allow him to go so far with helping her through this. "Okay. The next thing we need to talk about is who you're willing to tell that you're sick. I want to be able to call someone if I have to go out for a while. Just in case."

Sighing, Shelby ran a hand through her spikey hair. "I don't want everyone to know, but I'll call a few of the girls—Kristen, Angie, Kayla, and Charlotte. If I tell one, I have to tell the others. And you can let Devon, Ian, and Mitch know, but no one else for now, please."

"Okay." He snorted. "It took me a second to remember Charlotte is Mistress China's real name. I rarely hear anyone use it."

"Even though she's a Domme, we've become pretty good friends. She was great the night..." Shelby bit her bottom lip.

"The night my asshole brother hit you," he finished for her, reaching over to take her hand. "You have no idea how much I regret bringing him to the club."

Squeezing his hand, her expression softened. "It's not your fault, and it's in the past. But I'm glad he doesn't live in the area because I'd be tempted to take Charlotte's whip to him."

Parker snorted. "I'd tie him to a St. Andrew's cross for you."

A giggle escaped her, and a grin spread across his face. While the topic of conversation wasn't one he was thrilled with, the fact that she hadn't pulled her hand away had his heart filling with joy, and he would talk about anything as long as she touched him. Shelby looked right in his house—she made it seem more like a home.

He couldn't help himself. Tugging on her hand, he gently pulled her up and onto his lap. Her eyes narrowed warily, but she didn't object. While his gaze searched her face for a sign that this wasn't what she wanted, he cupped the back of her head and closed the distance between them. Her breath hitched, causing his cock to twitch. This was something he'd craved for so long—something he dreamed of—and he wasn't going to rush it. He groaned when her tongue peeked out to wet her pretty, pink lips. His words came out in a husky whisper. "Tell me you want me, baby. Ask me to kiss you."

His heart pounded in his chest as he waited for her answer.

CHAPTER SEVEN

Inhaling deeply, Shelby reveled in Parker's scent and the feel of his strong, solid body. Wetness pooled between her legs. A kiss. One kiss and she could die a happy woman. *No, damn it.* She could *live* a happy woman. She'd fought death before and won—she could do it again. Not only did she want to live, but she wanted what this man was offering her—even if it was only for a little while. She couldn't have forever with him, but she could have now.

"Please, kiss me, Sir."

The words were barely out of her mouth before he pressed his lips to hers. She could feel the tension in his body as he held himself back. Not wanting gentle, she nipped his bottom lip with her teeth. Parker snarled and plunged his tongue into her mouth. The beast in him was released, and she met it with the one inside her. Their tongues dueled as she shifted to straddle his lap. Kissing him was just as she'd suspected it would be—explosive. All thoughts of her cancer, chemotherapy, and anything else disappeared from her brain as she let her body take over the moment.

Changing the angle of his head, he devoured her. One hand held her head in place while the other closed around her breast. His heat scorched her, and her back bowed, thrusting her lush flesh further into his touch. Moans emanated from her, followed by a whimper when he pulled his mouth from hers.

Breathless, Parker held her to his chest. "Damn, that was better than I remembered it was, and you better believe I've dreamed of doing that since the last time I kissed you. But if I don't stop now, I won't be able to."

"What if I don't want to stop?" And she didn't want to. All she wanted was for him to keep kissing her and to fuck her with that rock-hard bulge in his pants.

He stiffened, and the fingers in her hair tightened just enough to give her a bite of pain. "Topping from the bottom, baby? You know better than that. And until I talk to your doctor tomorrow and have my list of questions answered, this is as far as I'm willing to go. You're important to me, Shelby, and I don't want to fuck up and do anything that might hurt you." Snorting, he ran a hand down her back. "Jeez, if someone told me two days ago that I would stop once

I had you in my arms, I would've told them they were crazy."

Resting her head on his shoulder, she placed a chaste kiss on his neck. This was so nice, sitting in his lap as if she belonged there. But she didn't. Sooner or later, she would have to tell him why she couldn't be his—why she couldn't stay.

How long they sat that way, content in the silence, she wasn't sure, but reality burst her bubble when his phone rang. Figuring it had to be about his work, Shelby slid out of his arms and stood. She picked up their plates and glasses, then carried them into the kitchen as he answered the phone. While she hadn't meant to eavesdrop, she couldn't help but hear his aggravated tone.

"Hello... We've been through this. I can't drop everything and run to Boston because you want me to. I have a business to run. A successful one, not that it makes any difference to you... I don't know when I'll be able to get up there... State Senate? Well, good for you... I don't know."

A growl came from the family room, and it hadn't been Spanky. "I said, I don't know... I have things to take care of down here... Well, they're important to me... Fine. I'll check my calendar... I said... Never mind... *Goodbye to you, too, Father.*"

The last sentence had been spat out sarcastically, and Shelby got the impression he'd been talking to dead air. His father had probably hung up. Poor Parker.

Not only was his brother an asshole, but his father also sounded like one. She didn't know anything about his family and hoped there was at least one person among them who was there for him because those two men obviously weren't.

She realized she was still standing there, frozen in place, and moved to put the plates in the dishwasher as he walked into the kitchen. "You don't have to do that. I'll clean up."

Cocking her hip, she scowled at him. "I'm not an invalid, Parker. If you insist that I stay with you during my chemo, then I insist on carrying my own weight around here."

In a blink of an eye, he was across the room, sweeping her into his arms. Laughing at her shocked expression, he held her close. "I think I like carrying your weight around, baby. And you're here to get better, not clean up. But if you want, maybe you can give me some decorating ideas. If you hadn't noticed, my place screams bachelor pad."

Beneath her, Spanky woofed loudly at their antics. Shelby giggled, loving the feeling of being in Parker's arms. "Yes, it does, and I would love to help you decorate. It'll give me something to do when I'm not sleeping or puking in the toilet."

Placing her back on her feet, he kissed the top of her head. "How are you feeling? Are you up for a walk with me and Spanky? There's a dog run in the park up the street, and he likes to go hang out with his best buds and lady friends. He's got the hots for this standard poodle who won't give him the time of day. But he keeps trying." Bending, he covered the big dog's ears with his hands. "Don't tell him he's been fixed. I don't think he's figured it out yet."

A full belly laugh burst from her lips. The man was entertaining in more ways than one. "I won't say a word. And a walk sounds great."

"Good. Why don't you put your sneakers on, and I'll grab his leash, ball, and poop bags—extra strength."

Shelby watched as he left the room with Spanky on his heels. Biting her lip, she tried to tell herself that this was only temporary. She would either move back to her condo when her chemo was done or... well, she didn't want to think of the alternative. Either way, she'd be leaving this wonderful man. But for now, she selfishly wanted him. She wanted to enjoy their time together while she still had a chance.

"Hi, Parker." The ladies greeted him in unison as he opened the front door. Kristen, Angie, Kayla, and Boomer's girlfriend, Kat Maier, followed Mistress China into the foyer.

"Hello, ladies. Head on back to the patio. Shelby's taking advantage of the comfortable weather."

It was the Thursday after her third treatment and a week since she'd moved in with him. The meeting with her doctor the previous Friday had gone well, and Parker had his list of questions answered to his satisfaction. He now knew all about her type of cancer, the course of treatment, the survival statistics—which, thankfully, were good—and what he could do to make everything a little easier for her.

She'd been a little fatigued that night, so he'd bundled her up on the couch and let her pick out a movie. Expecting it to be a chick-flick, he'd been pleasantly surprised to find out she was an action-movie lover like him, and they'd ended up having a *Die Hard* marathon. It'd been nice having her lay her head on a pillow in his lap as he stroked her hair and arm.

When she'd finally fallen asleep, he stayed that way for a while, loving the moment's intimacy. And that was almost as intimate as they'd been over the past few days, aside from a few chaste kisses and hugs. She no longer seemed uneasy about being with him, but he didn't want to push things when she didn't feel well.

On Monday, Parker ensured his foremen could handle things and told them to contact him by phone for emergencies only. Everything else could wait until after Shelby's chemotherapy session. He had to hand it to the staff at the treatment center—they were absolutely phenomenal. The nurses explained everything to them and answered any questions he thought of.

They ensured she was comfortable and made her laugh with silly stories and jokes.

While the drugs were slowly pumped into her system, a trained therapy dog had stopped by for a visit, and Shelby had taken a few minutes to talk with the handler while scratching the Golden Retriever's ears. If one had to go through chemo, that was the place to do it. Even the décor was soothing.

Taking her doctor's advice, he'd filled his refrigerator and pantry with healthy foods and nutritional supplements. Ginger ale, tea, and candies were stocked for when her nausea hit. He made sure she walked with him for exercise when she felt up to it and slept when she needed it.

Spanky had become her guardian and Parker's alert system. If he was in his home office or somewhere else in the house and Shelby dashed to the bathroom to get sick, the Bullmastiff barked until Parker came running. Then, the canine and his master would stay with her until her stomach stopped rebelling against the chemo drugs in her system. And like his owner, Spanky would use his body for Shelby to lean on when she was feeling weak. The dog was never far from her side.

Today, Parker had planned to work from home, but Kristen had called earlier to say they were coming over for a visit since Shelby was having a low-nausea day and felt up to having visitors. Once he made sure they didn't need anything and knew to call him if her symptoms changed, he'd go to the office and a few job sites to see if everything was running smoothly. He had a great bunch of workers, but he was still the owner. If things went wrong, they were his responsibility, whether he had been on-site or not.

"Parker, I love your house. It's beautiful inside and out," Angie gushed. "Ian said you renovated it, but I didn't expect this."

During the renovations, he incorporated elements of nature into the design of the patio. A river-rock fireplace was on one side of the sitting area, and a matching outdoor kitchen with a built-in barbecue was on the opposite end. Instead of having a tin roof or retractable awning, a large portion of the patio was covered in a stained, teak canopy.

The in-ground pool had been created to mimic a small pond, complete with a rock waterfall. Trees and foliage helped make it a tropical paradise. This was the one part of the house he'd decorated nicely with comfortable sitting areas and strategically placed lighting for when the sun went down. It was his and Spanky's favorite part of the house.

"Thanks. But I need help with decorating the inside. Shelby's been making notes about what I need to buy so it doesn't scream bachelor pad." Before they'd gotten there, he'd set out a pitcher of lemonade and a vegetable platter with dip. Now, he pointed to the kitchen area. "There are plenty of other drinks and snacks in there, along with glasses, bowls, and stuff. If you need anything else, feel free to raid the indoor kitchen."

Turning to Shelby, he asked, "Do you need anything before I go?"

Smiling, she shook her head. "Nope. I think we've got everything. Thanks."

"Great." He hesitated and then thought, "What the hell." Striding over to where she was sitting on a lounge chair, he leaned over and captured her lips with his own. Her breath hitched, but she didn't pull away. When he broke the kiss, her cheeks were stained red, and the pulse in her neck was pounding. Satisfaction coursed through him. "Have a nice visit with your friends. If you need me, call my cell, and I'll come right home."

"Okay."

The word came out in a soft whisper, and it thrilled him, knowing he was the reason she was breathless. Standing erect again, he nodded at the others. "Have fun, but make sure she doesn't overdo things."

Charlotte narrowed her eyes and teased him. "Honestly, Parker. We're not taking her out for shots and dirty dancing. We're saving that for tomorrow night."

The others laughed as Parker rolled his eyes. "Right. Sorry. I've gotten a little overprotective the past few days. Have a good time."

Convinced they would take good care of Shelby, he

left them to whatever women did when they got together like this.

As Parker cut through the house to the front door, Shelby's five friends stared at her in open curiosity. Her blush deepened. "Um. Does anyone want iced tea instead of lemonade?"

"Oh, no, you don't, Shelby." Kayla wagged a finger at her, then picked up the pitcher. "I'll get everyone's drinks while you start dishing about Master Parker and that hubba-hubba kiss he just gave you. And don't leave out a single naughty detail."

She bit her lip, then shrugged. "There's nothing to tell."

"Bullshit. Don't make me get my whip, Shelby." The expression on Charlotte's face said Mistress China was making an appearance.

Knowing there was no way around it, she released a deep breath and filled them in. "Okay. To tell you the truth, I have no idea what's going on. I mean... we haven't played or anything. We've only kissed a few times."

"But he wants more," Angie stated with confidence. "And so do you."

"But I can't." How could she explain this without telling them everything? They were her friends and would understand, but they would also tell her she was being crazy. "I can't be what he wants... what he needs. He needs a sub who can be a wife, and I'm not wife material."

"What?" Kristen crossed her arms and stared at her. "What the hell are you talking about? You'd make a great wife... and we aren't telling you to marry the guy if you don't want to. Just have some fun for a while... see where it goes."

Kayla handed her a glass. "Exactly. You know the lifestyle better than anyone. Negotiate a contract with the man. Put an end date on it, so no one has false expectations."

As the others added their input, Shelby eyed the silent Kat. Everyone was so glad she and Boomer had worked things out because they'd been in love with each other since they were teens, but a cruel fate had forced them to be separated for many years. Shelby still didn't know her that well, but what she did know, she liked.

Kat raised an eyebrow and smiled when she noticed Shelby staring at her. "What? You look like you want to ask me something."

"If I'm out of line, tell me. But if you hadn't needed Boomer's help, would you have come back to him? What I mean is... you two seem so perfect for one another. But would you've stayed away because there was a risk of causing him pain and possibly having him turn you away?"

The others all quieted and regarded Kat, who tilted her head in thought. "I'm not sure what my situation has to do with yours, but I don't mind telling you about it. After I started coming out of the shock of everything that'd happened back then, I went to bed every night, dreaming of someday being reunited with Benny. I never stopped loving him. Circumstances may have forced my hand in coming to him sooner than I was ready to, but I know I would've figured out a way to try to be together with him again."

She gave a small smile. "I would've preferred he didn't faint on me, but yeah... I would have come back either way. He told me that, for years, he debated that saying, 'Is it better to have loved and lost than never to have loved at all?' We both agree now it's better to have loved... because a life without love isn't a life at all."

Silence filled the air until Kayla let out a loud sniffle. "That's so fucking beautiful—I think I'm going to cry."

Everyone looked at her and burst out laughing when they realized she was teasing. Kristen tossed a throw pillow at her. "Oh, shut up. You know darn well that was incredibly romantic."

Shelby's shoulders relaxed as everyone started talking and joking with each other. Parker had been right—she needed her friends to get her through this. Kat was also right—a life without love really wasn't a life at all. And Shelby wanted to choose life... and love.

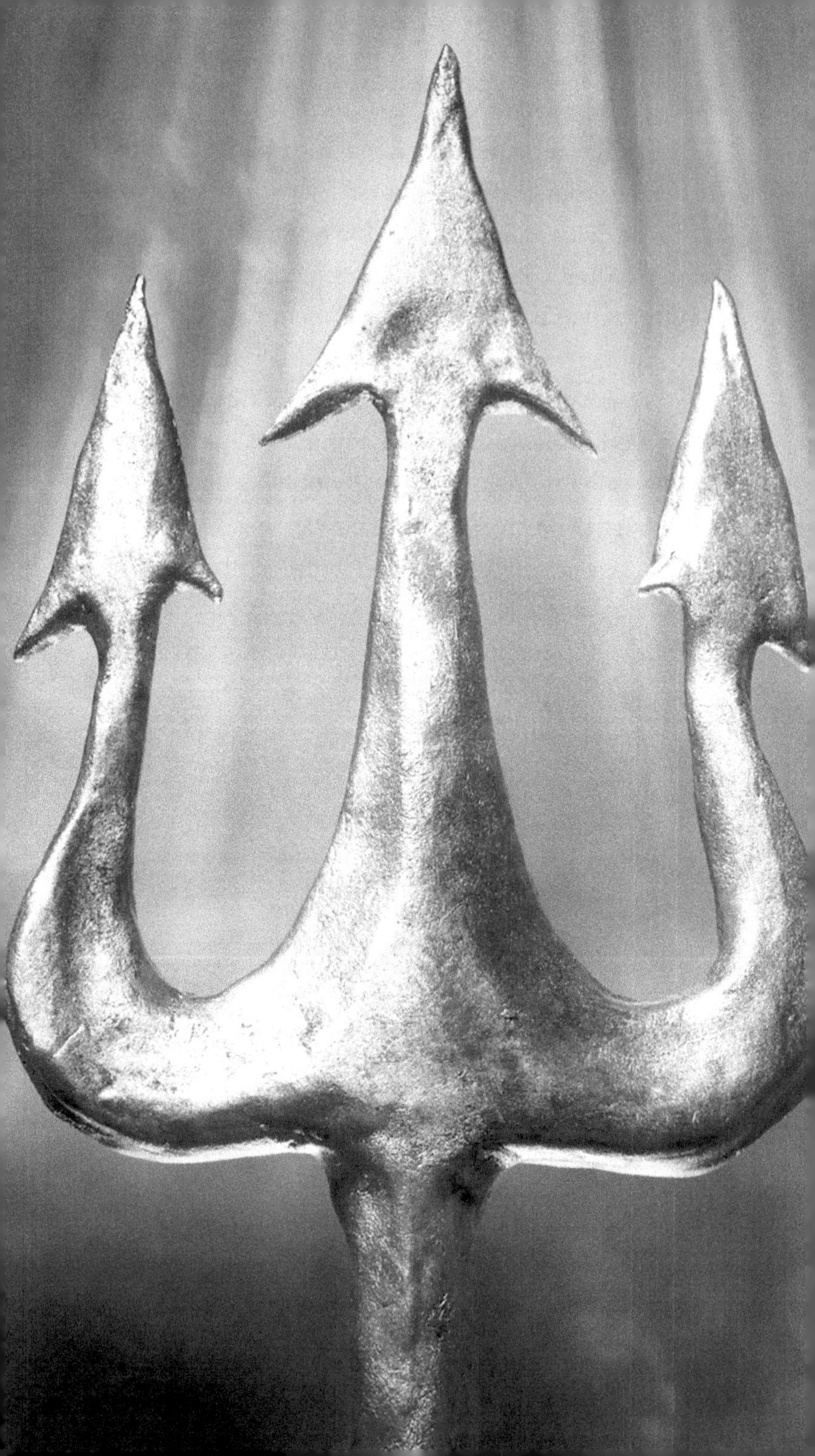

CHAPTER EIGHT

"A re you sure about this?"

While Spanky lay at her feet, Parker stood behind her in the master bathroom, where she sat in the chair he'd brought in. Her gaze met his in the mirror, and she nodded. "Yes, I'm sure. Every time I shower or run my fingers through it, more hair falls out. I'd rather look like I'm trying a new fashion statement than the sick chick losing her hair to chemo."

A scowl came across his face as he squeezed her shoulder. "You're not a 'sick chick.' You're a brave woman fighting an ugly disease and remaining beautiful as you kick its ass."

She blushed as she always did when he said things like that. Damn, this man was good for her ego as well as her spirits. She'd done the bald thing years ago, which was how her colored wig collection had started, but she was beautiful in Parker's eyes no matter how she appeared. "Thanks. Okay. Let's get this over with. Shave away."

It didn't take long for him to run the electric shaver over her head, and, unlike the first time she'd done this, she didn't cry. Standing and turning her head from side to side, she eyed her reflection. "At least I still have my eyebrows, so far. Last time, I had to use an eyebrow pencil to fill them in."

She turned to him and was surprised when he handed her the shaver and sat in the chair. "What are you doing?"

"It's my turn. With my receding hairline, I've been thinking about how I'd look bald. Think I can be the next Bruce Willis?"

Now, her eyes filled as she stepped behind the chair and stared at him in the mirror. Her voice cracked. "Y-you don't have to do this."

"It's not a matter of *having to*, baby. It's a *wanting-to* thing. Shave away."

She smiled as he repeated her earlier words. What had she ever done in her life to deserve a man like this? Ever since the girls' visit yesterday, she'd been thinking a lot about the two of them as a couple. Maybe she was selling herself short or underestimating him. Perhaps it wouldn't matter to him that she couldn't have kids.

Flipping the switch on the shaver, she brought it up and carefully started at his forehead. Gliding it along his scalp, she ensured she didn't miss a spot.

When she finished, Parker ran his hands over it. "Not bad at all. I think I like it better than the crewcut."

"It's sexy on you."

He raised an eyebrow. "Sexy?"

Her blush returned as she unplugged the razor and placed it in the drawer where Parker kept it. Apparently, letting her off the hook, he stood and grabbed the broom and dustpan he'd brought in. She moved the chair out of his way, and Spanky followed her to the kitchen as she returned the seat to where it belonged.

Biting her lip, she noticed the contract they'd signed the day she'd moved in lying on the kitchen table. The contract that said, "No sex."

Taking a leap of courage, she picked it up along with a pen and marched back to the master bathroom. He was flushing their mixed pile of hair down the toilet.

"I want to renegotiate, Sir."

Parker froze. His gaze moved from her face to the paper she held and back again. When he paled a little, she realized he thought something was wrong, and she hurried to reassure him. "I'd like to renegotiate item number five."

She handed him the paper and watched as he read the clause she was talking about. His eyes whipped up to hers again. "And what would you like to change number five to?"

"I'd like to eliminate it from the contract alto-gether, Sir."

Parker was dumbfounded. Surely, he hadn't heard her correctly. Number five was the clause about no sex. But the expression on her face said he hadn't misunderstood her. The desire he saw in her eyes made his heart soar and his cock swell. Swallowing hard, he dropped his voice into its commanding Dom tone. "Are you sure about this, baby? I know your doctor said there were no activities you couldn't do as long as you took it easy."

Certain things on her limit list would be out because she bruised easily now. The anemia that usually came with chemotherapy caused that. But there were a few things on her list they could do that would bring both of them pleasure. He knew because he'd seen her limit list at the club and practically memorized it.

Stepping forward, she took the paper back and crossed off number five. "I'm sure about it, Master Parker."

God, the woman humbled him and drove him insane simultaneously. Glancing down, he noticed Spanky at Shelby's heels. "Outside, Spanky. We don't want an audience."

As the dog reluctantly left, Parker pulled Shelby into his arms. Even bald, she was the most beautiful woman in the world to him, and her body molded to his like they'd been made for each other. "You'll tell me if things get too much for you, and you will obey me. Any questions?"

Her breathing hitched as she reached up with one hand and caressed his cheek. "Just one, Sir. When are you going to kiss me again?"

Have mercy.

Crushing his mouth to hers, he held her tighter against him. And he never wanted to let her go again. Someway somehow, she would be his and his alone. His tongue probed her sweet lips, and he rejoiced when she allowed him entry to her mouth. Trying to be gentle was so difficult when what he truly wanted was to fuck her into oblivion.

Sliding his hands down her body, he cupped her ass and lifted her off the floor. Her legs wrapped around his hips, and his cock nestled against her mound as he walked them into the bedroom, where he set her on her feet again. He couldn't stop kissing her —didn't want to—but there were things he wanted even more. Pulling away, he smiled at her mumbled protest.

"Undress for me, baby. I want to watch you strip for me."

"Yes, Sir."

God, he loved hearing that from her lips. Maybe

soon, she would be calling him Master. Not just Master Parker but *her* Master.

Sitting on the edge of the bed, he leaned back on his elbows, watching her. And Shelby didn't disappoint him. While dressed in Hello Kitty lounge pants and a matching shirt, she was still incredibly sexy. Swaying her hips to a tune only she heard, she gazed at him seductively and slowly lifted her shirt, teasing him inch by inch. When the hem reached just below her breasts, she spun around and gave him her back while smirking at him over her shoulder.

Little brat.

Parker didn't bother to hide his need to adjust himself. He was hard and throbbing, and she knew it. Lifting the T-shirt over her head, she tossed it aside before turning around again with her hands covering her breasts. He licked his lips. "Let me see them, baby. Play with those pretty pink nipples that I can't wait to suck into my mouth."

Shelby moaned but did as she was told. It was the sexiest thing he'd ever seen. Her thumbs and forefingers closed around the stiff peaks and tugged on them. Her hips were still undulating, and he crocked a finger at her to come closer. "Don't stop playing."

He sat forward and pulled on the tie at her waist. The loose pants fell to her feet, leaving her naked since she hadn't been wearing underwear, and he stared at the feminine paradise in front of him. She was waxed bare like she normally was at the club, and he was dying to find out if she tasted as good as he dreamed she would.

His gaze lifted to hers, and she held her breath as he brought a hand up between her legs. "Open for me, baby."

She spread her legs wider and waited. Teasing her, he ran a finger up her thigh, over her mound, and back down the other leg. Repeating the process again and again, he restrained himself from moving too fast. "Tell me. Are you wet for me, Shelby?"

"Y-yes, Sir."

The quiver in her voice pleased the Dom in him. "Should I see for myself how wet you are?"

"Oh God, please, Sir. Yes."

Instead of running his own fingers through her folds, he took her right hand and brought it to her core. He pressed on her fingers, dragged them through her moisture, then lifted them to his mouth. His tongue darted out and licked the wet digits. "Fuck, baby, you're delicious."

Sucking her fingers into his mouth, he cleaned them off one by one. He tugged on her hips until she lay on the bed next to him. Sliding off the bed, he knelt between her legs and tucked his hands under her ass. "Get comfy, baby. Keep your hands above your head, no squirming, and no coming until I say so. This will take a while before I've had my fill."

Oh. My. God. If she'd known Parker was so damn talented with his tongue, she would've buckled a long time ago. Above her head, Shelby fisted the comforter in her hands as she tried to keep her hips still. His thumb brushed over her clit, and a gasp burst from her lips. He hadn't been lying when he said he would take his time. Again and again, he licked and sucked on her folds before impaling her with his stiffened tongue.

In and out.

Up and over.

Side to side.

Swirl around.

Thrust.

Repeat.

"Oh, yes! Sir, that feels so good. Please. Mmmooorrrre."

He smiled against her mound at her pleading before his mouth inched upward and gave her clit some attention while one finger, then two, eased into her wet pussy. She was panting now, and her heart pounded in her chest. Slowly, he took her higher and higher, and each time she thought she had reached the peak, she found there was more climbing to do. His fingers didn't stop their sensual assault when he kissed his way up her abdomen, joining her on the bed. The licking and sucking continued on one nipple and then the other. Electricity hummed throughout her body.

"You don't know how long I've dreamed of this, Shelby." He nuzzled her breasts, her shoulders, her neck. "I want you to come for me. I want you to shatter around my fingers first and then again around my cock. Come for me, baby."

He picked up the pace as his fingertips searched for that spot. The one that would send her over the edge. A little more. Oh, shit, she was almost there... almost. "Please," she begged a split second before the wave rushed within her, sending her spiraling into the abyss. She'd played with many Doms over the years, experiencing orgasms easily, but never like this. It was beyond anything she'd ever felt before.

Her body tensed and quivered as another orgasm crashed behind the first. An involuntary scream emanated from her throat moments before Parker covered her mouth with his own, claiming her release in every way possible. How was she going to let this man go after this?

He eased up as she floated back down, gasping for air. "Holy shit."

Kissing the swells of her breasts, he chuckled. "Damn, that was beautiful, baby. I can't wait to feel what you just did to my fingers when you do it around my cock."

"Neither can I, Sir. Please, don't make either of us wait."

"Ha! I think you barely missed topping from the bottom with that, my little subbie. But I'm too fucking hungry for you to analyze it." Parker pulled his fingers from her core and reached over to the nightstand next to his bed, retrieving a condom from the drawer. She wished she dared to tell him protection wasn't necessary, but she didn't. Condoms were mandatory in the club, and she hadn't had sex outside The Covenant in years. And physicals, including blood work and STD testing, were also required every six months to keep one's play privileges. She knew she was clean, and most likely he was too, but until they compared notes later, a condom was necessary. But they didn't need to get into it now.

Shelby watched as Parker stripped off his T-shirt, worn jeans, and boxer briefs. Her breath caught at the sight of his hard shaft. Damn, the man was hung. How had she not known how big he was?

Because, you idiot, you refused to play with him before and always avoided watching his scenes so you could keep him at arm's length.

She told her inner voice to shut the hell up as she watched him roll on the rubber casing. Too bad he seemed as desperate to get inside her as she was to have him there because she would've liked to take the time to explore that gorgeous cock with her mouth and tongue.

Stepping between her legs draped over the side of the bed, his gaze held hers. "Back up on the bed, baby, and spread those pretty legs for me."

She did as she was told, then licked her lips as Parker knelt between her thighs. Lining the tip of his cock with her slit, he tilted his hips forward, cautiously entering her. She knew he was going slow for several reasons but wished he would throw them out the window and fuck her hard and fast. But then it would be over too soon, so maybe slow was good. Her core yielded to the natural invasion, and she moaned with every drag of his hard, thick flesh against her walls.

With each small thrust, he made his way further and further until every inch was buried inside of her. "Fuck! Baby, you're so fucking tight. Don't move. Shit, don't move. Let me… let me get some control here. Otherwise, this will be over in seconds."

His body was rigid as he fought his release. Finally, with elbows on either side of her head, he started to pull out and plunge back into her. He filled her in more ways than one. Not only was he filling her body, but her heart, mind, and soul, as well. If she wasn't careful, she could fall in love with this man.

Oh, who the fuck am I kidding, I'm already halfway there.

Increasing the pace, he fucked her harder and harder with each stroke. She gasped and moaned with each slap of his pelvis against her clit. She was back up on that cliff, ready to fall again. Parker bent his head to her breasts, licking her nipples. "Come for me, Shelby. Take me over the edge with you." He bit down all one of her straining peaks, and that's all it took for her to spiral into oblivion, dragging him with her.

As their orgasms ebbed, they struggled to catch their breaths. Parker eased out of her, and she whimpered at the loss of contact. He climbed from the bed and disposed of the condom in the bathroom before returning to cuddle her against him. They lay naked atop the comforter, content in a few moments of silence.

He kissed her cheek. "Are you okay, baby? Go to sleep if you want."

Nestling closer to his chest, she pressed her lips to his neck. "I'm more than okay. If I sleep, will you stay with me?"

"Of course. But before you drift off, I have a request. Unlike my other demands, this one is negotiable."

She lifted her head so she could see his face. "What?"

"I want you to be my sub, Shelby. I want you to wear my collar. At least, while you're staying with me. I want everyone to know that, for now, you're mine. We can negotiate and amend the contract after your nap. Will you think about it?"

Holy shit! She should have seen this coming. All the

signs were there, but she'd hoped he would be satisfied with their contract the way it was written.

Well, you're the one who amended it first.

Could she do it? Why not? He'd been wonderful, taking care of her. This would be a way she could thank him for everything he was doing for her. A collar wasn't forever. When she was done with her chemo and no longer needed his help, she could return it without consequences—except maybe a broken heart. But his happiness was worth any future heartache.

Reaching up, she stroked his cheek. "I'd be honored to wear your collar, Master."

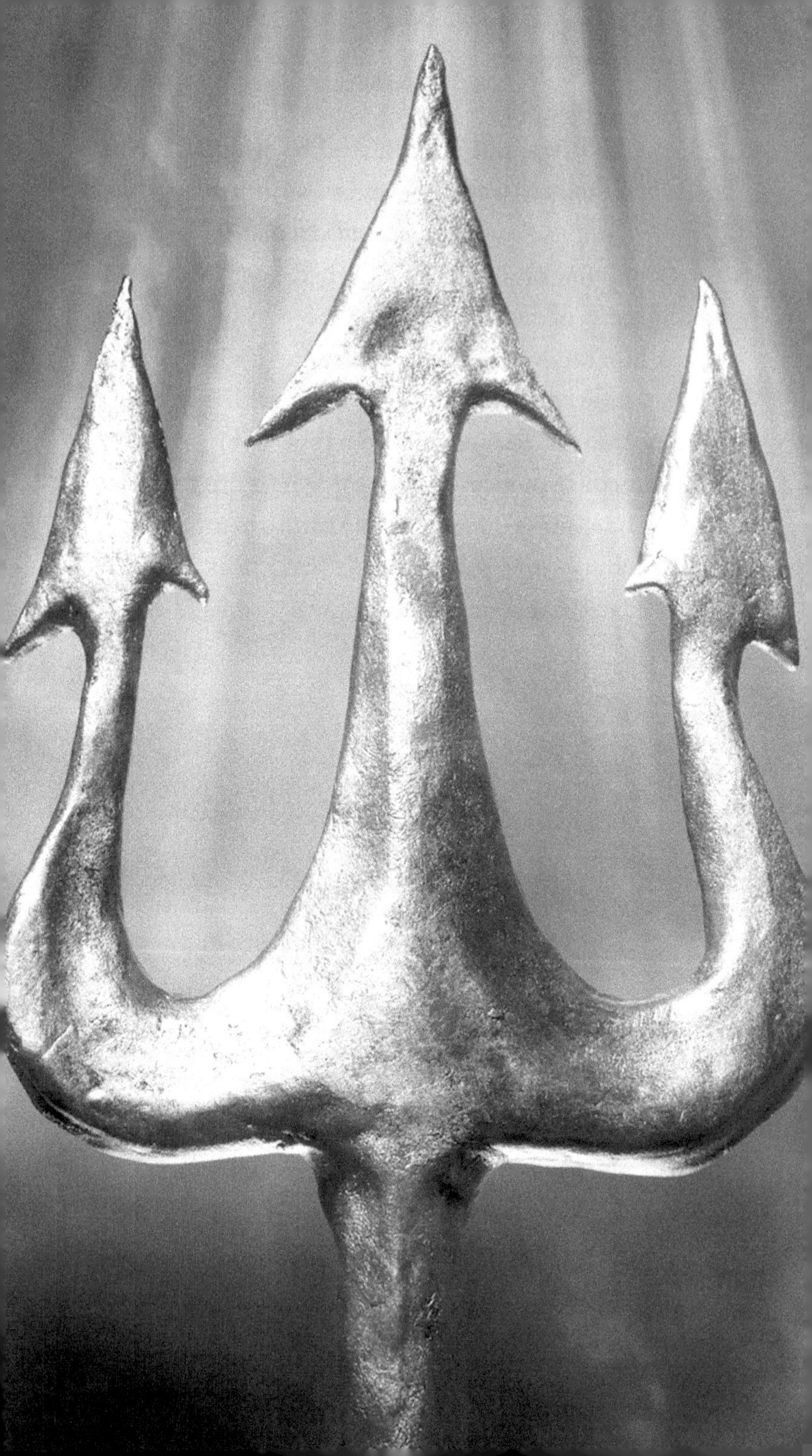

CHAPTER NINE

Parker held Shelby's elbow as she climbed the stairs to the second-floor entrance of the club. As usual for a Friday night, the parking lot was packed. While she was feeling a little fatigued, she wanted to come and thank everyone for their support. Word had gotten out about her cancer, but she didn't mind. The club members had all been wonderful, bringing food to Parker's for them, picking up her mail, watering her plants, or just plain making her smile and laugh.

She had one more round of treatment to go, and then came the testing to see if she needed more. God, she hoped not. She wanted time to recover for Devon and Kristen's wedding. As it was, she'd lost some weight and had gone to the bridal shop yesterday with Kristen to get her bridesmaid dress altered to fit again. Whether she could make the reception or not, she was determined to be there as the couple exchanged wedding vows. After all, she'd been the one to tell Kristen about the club when the author was researching BDSM for her next romance novel. The tour she'd arranged was where Devon and Kristen's love story began.

Stopping at the top of the stairs, she caught her breath. Parker had offered to carry her up, but she wanted to do it on her own.

"You okay?"

She nodded her head, and the lime green tresses of her wig bounced around her shoulders. While Parker had insisted she wear a comfortable yet fashionable sweat suit to stay warm, she hadn't wanted to show off her bald head to everyone, even though her close friends had already seen it. Besides, she was known for wearing her colored wigs, so it wouldn't appear weird to anyone here. "Yeah, I'm good."

"Promise me you'll let me know if it's too much and you want to go home. I'll have you out of here in a flash."

"I will. And Parker, thanks for everything you've done for me. I can't say that enough."

Taking her hand, he brought it to his lips. "It's been my absolute pleasure, baby."

And that was the truth for her as well. It had been an absolute pleasure being with him. Not only had they shared the same bed since the day he'd shaved her head, but they had gotten to know each other more in every way.

Their walks with Spanky and evenings sitting on the patio had been their time to talk about everything under the sun. They filled each other in with stories of their youths and adulthood, how they both started in the BDSM lifestyle and what was on their bucket lists. They discussed movies, books, art, politics, and current events. The only thing Shelby regretted was that she hadn't gotten to know this man sooner. That had been her fault, but she hoped she was making up for it now.

Parker opened the door, and they walked in. She was surprised to see no one at the front desk or guarding the entrance. In fact, there was no one in the lobby at all. She glanced up at him. "Where is everyone?"

Shrugging, he walked to the antique wood and iron doors that led into the club. "Don't know. Inside, I guess."

When the door opened and she stepped inside, Shelby's jaw hit the floor.

"Surprise!"

Oh. My. God. The bar area was packed, with everyone cheering and clapping for her. And the men... *holy crap*... the men, and one or two of the women, were bald, or almost bald. Tears filled her eyes as Ian, Devon, and Mitch stepped toward her. They had all done this for her.

Ian reached her first and kissed her cheek. "Hey, sweetheart. No tears." He thumbed away the first ones that fell. "We all wanted to show you how much we love you and are here for you."

Pushing his brother out of the way, Devon took his place and hugged her. "You better believe we love you, honey. I haven't been this bald since I entered BUD/s training. I don't shave my head for just anyone. And before I forget, Masters Jake and Marco send their best, but they're out of town on an assignment and couldn't be here tonight. But they'll see you when they get home."

Devon released her into Mitch's arms. "I've never been this bald unless you count when I was born." After he kissed her forehead, he gave her a mocking frown. "And just so you know, I'm still planning on punishing you somehow for not telling us what was going on in the first place. Our lives are much brighter with you in it, and we'll always be here for you."

Shelby was a sobbing mess as others formed a line to greet her and pledge their support. Angie, Kristen, Kat, Boomer, Brody, Kayla, and her wife, Roxy, Tiny, and Carter were the first ones in line. It wasn't until the latter approached her that she realized he was the only guy in the place still with his hair.

After kissing her on the cheek, Master Carter ran a hand through his long, dark-blond tresses. "I'm sorry, little one, but I needed to keep this scruff for work." He waggled his eyebrows. "But if you want, I can man-scape to compensate for it. I'll even trust you with the razor if you want to do it for me."

All she knew about the man's job was that he worked for the government and he had to disappear for weeks at a time. Giggles escaped her at his teasing, but next to her, Parker growled. "I'd be more than happy to take a razor to your crotch, jackass. If you hadn't noticed, she's wearing my collar now."

Carter barked out a laugh and clapped the other man on the shoulder. "Oh, I noticed. Just wanted to get a rise out of you. You're too fucking easy, Park." He winked at Shelby. "If he gets out of line, you let me know."

Smiling at Parker, she answered the other Dom. "I will. But I don't think I have to worry about that. He treats me like a princess."

"As he should, sweetheart. As he should."

The next hour was a blur as scores of members hugged and kissed her as she sat on a stool at the bar. Not once did Parker leave her side. Every ten minutes or so, he'd whisper in her ear, asking if she was doing okay or if she wanted to go home. While another woman might have felt he was smothering her, Shelby was grateful he cared enough to check on her. She would have been lost and miserable these past few weeks if he hadn't been there for her. And somewhere along the line, she'd fallen in love with him. But was that enough?

Tonight. When they got home tonight, she would tell him the only secret that stood between them and pray it didn't make a difference to him. She would pray that if her cancer went into remission, he wouldn't let her go back to her lonely condo. Parker Christiansen hadn't just gotten under her skin. He had burrowed deep into her heart, where she knew he would remain until the day she died—whether that was in the near future or fifty years from now.

Parker locked the back doors after Spanky finished his outdoor business and returned to the house. It was a little after eleven, and he'd been surprised that Shelby had lasted that long at the club. Well, not really, since he'd kept her activity to a minimum. They'd spent most of the evening sitting at the bar. He hadn't wanted her to walk around and get too fatigued.

He'd been as shocked as she had been at the room of bald heads. No one had told him they were doing it, but the outpouring of support for Shelby told him he'd made the right decision about having her let the others know about her cancer.

Turning at a noise behind him, he found her taking a seat on the couch. She was still dressed but had removed her wig. "You should be getting ready for bed. You have to be exhausted."

She patted the seat next to her. "I'm good for now. But I want to talk to you about something first."

His stomach sank as he sat. He didn't like the way she had said that. "Okay. What's up?"

Shelby twisted her hands together, and her nervousness ate at his gut. He was about to ask her what was wrong when she leaped from the couch and began to pace the room. "I have to tell you something, but I'm not sure how you'll take it. These past few weeks with you have been amazing—better than I ever thought they could be—well, despite the big 'C,' of course. And I think..."

She stopped in front of him and fingered the simple, black leather collar he'd given her to wear until he could pick out something prettier. Inhaling deeply, she let it out just as fast. "No—not I *think*—I *know* I've fallen in love with you."

What? That was so not what he expected her to say. *Holy fuck!* He stood and placed his hands on her shoulders. "Say—say that again, please. It kinda sounded like you said you were in love with me... and I really hope that's what you did say."

"I'm in love with you." This time, it was said in a sexy whisper, but the words came through loud and clear.

Parker picked her up in his arms and spun her around before kissing the hell out of her. When he tried to deepen the kiss, however, she pulled away.

"Parker, wait—"

"Wait, what?" Why was she stopping? His mind replayed her words, and it was then that he realized he hadn't said the words back to her yet. *You dumb fuck!* "I love you too, Shelby. I think I fell in love with you a long time ago."

He lowered his head to capture her lips again, but she pushed on his chest. "Parker, please. There's something else I need to tell you."

The seriousness in her gaze and voice had him reeling in his desire. He took a step back and gave her some room. "Okay. What is it?" Tears filled her eyes as she bit her bottom lip, and he reached up to pop it free. "You can tell me anything, baby. After telling me you love me, nothing else you can say will change how I feel about you. Tell me."

"I—I can't have children." His eyes narrowed in concern at her unsteady voice, but he let her continue. "My cancer seven years ago was ovarian. It resulted in them being removed along with a hysterectomy. It's why I never wanted to play with you at the club before. I knew I could easily fall in love with you, but you're the type of guy who deserves a wife and kids and grandkids. And..."

He was stunned and hurt. "And you thought I'd turn you away because you can't have kids? Seriously? Did you honestly think I was that shallow?"

"No! No, Parker. I—I just thought you deserved someone better than me. Someone who could give you what I couldn't."

"Aw, Shelby. Baby." He pulled her back into his arms. How much time together had they missed because of her insecurities? "How could you ever think that? I'm the one who's worried you deserve someone better than me. I don't know how to be a good husband and father—I didn't have a good role model growing up. My folks were more concerned about their social lives than their sons. The household staff were more loving to us than our parents were. And so what if you can't give birth to our children? There are other options like surrogates or adoption. Blood doesn't make you a good mother. The love you give a child does that. I love you, baby, and as I said before, nothing you say will change that."

She gazed up at him with watery eyes. "Make love to me, Master?"

Cupping her chin, he stared at her, knowing what she was really asking. Her use of his title indicated that she wanted him to take control—to dominate her. But the other words meant something more. They had started as friends who became D/s "play" partners. Tonight, it would go beyond that. Tonight, they would become lovers in every sense of the word.

Bending his knees, he picked her up in his arms and carried her to their bedroom. The trust in her eyes humbled him. She was giving him her heart, her love, and her world, and he would cherish each one.

Placing her on her feet next to the bed, he wordlessly removed her clothes and then his own. When they were both naked, he asked, "Should I get my toy bag, baby? Can you handle that? I promise I'll go easy, just a few toys to give you pleasure."

Shelby nodded. "I love and trust you. Do whatever you wish, Master."

"I love that word from your lips. And I love you, too. Lie down in the middle of the bed, and I'll be right back." He turned toward the door and groaned. "Honestly, Spanky, we don't need an audience for this. Come on, I'll get you a treat."

The big goofball stood in the doorway with his head cocked, but the word treat had him sprinting into the kitchen. Parker chuckled when the dog met him in the foyer and dropped his treat jar on the floor. He fished out a bone-shaped biscuit and handed it over before grabbing his toy bag from the closet. Shortly after Shelby had moved in, he took inventory of the bag and ensured he had everything he would need if she agreed to play with him.

Leaving Spanky crunching away, he carried the black duffel back to the bedroom. Seeing Shelby lying seductively across the bed had him harder than he'd been all night. Damn, she was beautiful.

"Spread your arms and legs, baby."

She didn't question why. She just did as he'd ordered. The heat in her eyes had to be reflected in his own. As he walked around the foot of the bed, his gaze went to her bare pussy, which was already glistening with moisture—for him. He couldn't wait to feast on her, but first things first.

He made quick work of attaching restraints to the bed and shackling her wrists, so she was at his mercy. A double-check of each one revealed he hadn't made them too tight. Her iron levels were still in the anemic range, so he had to be careful not to bruise her. "Comfy, baby?"

"Yes, Sir."

"Good." He pulled a few more items out of his bag and placed them on the bed before dropping the duffel on the floor. "Bend your legs and put your feet on the bed."

When she obeyed his command, he climbed between her knees and reached for a tube of lubricant. As far as he knew, it had been a long time since anyone had fucked her ass, if ever. The scenes and ménages he'd seen her participate in at the club were always a combination of oral and pussy sex. But anal plugs were a different story. He knew she enjoyed those. Maybe someday she would let him fuck her back hole, but for tonight, a new vibrating plug would fill her there. She watched as he opened the package and covered the toy's tip with lube.

Spreading her ass cheeks, he ran the tip over her puckered rosette, causing her to moan. "Like that, baby?"

"Yes, Sir."

"Then you're going to like this even more."

He added pressure, pushing the tip in, and was elated to see her pussy grow wetter. With short strokes, he advanced the plug until her hole closed around the narrowest part. Flipping the small switch, he turned it on, and Shelby gasped. "Oh, shit!"

Knowing the nerves in her ass were being lit up, he grinned and stood again. This time, he restrained her ankles so she was spread eagle in front of him. He watched her hips squirm and fisted his cock. "Can't wait to get inside of you, baby, but I'll have to. There is so much more I want to do to you before then. Close your eyes."

He picked up the short flogger and walked around to the side of the bed. With a gentle hand, he let the strands of leather fall onto her breasts. Her moans told him she wanted it harder, but until she was feeling better, that wasn't an option. Peppering her torso with soft strikes, he worked the flogger from her chest to her mound and back again. Whenever he hit her clit and pussy, she begged for more but kept her eyes shut. "Please, more, Sir. Oh, shit, right there. Yes!"

Her skin began to flush a light pink shade, and her nipples hardened for him. Tossing aside the flogger, he bent over and sucked one of the rigid peaks in his mouth while his hand glided down her abdomen to her clit. Mimicking what his tongue and teeth were doing to her nipple, his fingers brushed over the exposed little nub and pinched it.

Her cries of need and want urged him on. Letting her tit go with a pop, he leaned across her body, so his mouth could close around her other one and give it the same attention. His fingers slid further between her legs and found she was soaked for him. Running the tips between her pussy lips, he curled his fingers into her and felt her restraint to keep from thrusting her hips upward. *Such a good little subbie.*

The vibrator in her ass made the walls of her sex quiver as he fucked her with his fingers. Her pleadings went up an octave when he found her G-spot and rubbed it vigorously. His need to be inside her grew. "Come for me, baby. Come for me, and then I'll let you take my cock."

Her body tensed, then splintered apart. Screams of pleasure filled the air as the orgasm rolled through her in waves. Seeing her come for him was the most incredible sight—one he wanted to see every day for the rest of his life.

As she settled back down, he reached for the night-stand drawer for a condom, but her raspy voice stopped him. "Please, Sir, don't. I want to feel you. We're both clean and don't have to worry about pregnancy. Please?"

His cock stiffened to the point of pain. He'd never gone bareback in his life. They'd both had their bi-annual, club-mandated physicals within the past few weeks and had only been with each other since. Taking her with no barrier was something he wanted more than anything else.

Instead of digging into the drawer, he reached over and began to undo her restraints. He needed her hands on him when they made love. Playtime was over, and passion had taken its place. Removing the anal plug, he dropped it on his T-shirt, sitting atop the pile of clothes on the floor. Climbing on the bed, he told her, "Move over, baby. I want you on top, riding me."

They switched places, and she straddled his hips, her eyes full of love and desire. He'd never seen her like this before... this was a Shelby he hoped no one had ever seen before. She was in love... with him... and he was the luckiest man alive because of it.

Wrapping her hand around his shaft, she guided him into her. It was pure heaven. He wanted to sear this moment into his brain so that, fifty years from now, he could still recall the first time there had been nothing between them. Using her hands on his chest for support, she lowered herself at an excruciatingly slow rate until he was finally buried deep inside her core. Wet, scorching heat surrounded him. His eyes rolled back in his head as she started to lift herself back up. "Damn, baby, this is incredible. You're incredible. Ride me, baby."

His hands clutched her hips, and together, they found a rhythm that soon had them spiraling out of control. Brushing his thumbs against the sides of her clit, he drove her higher and higher. She had to come first—she would always come first in his life. He thrust into her, imprinting himself on her body. She was his now. His submissive. His love. And one day, his wife.

"Now, baby! Come for me now!"

Throwing her head back, she shattered around him, taking him over the edge seconds later. *Holy shit.* He couldn't stop coming as he emptied his seed inside her. Her fingers curled into his chest, leaving scratch marks he would wear with honor. He loved that she was marking him.

Gasping for air, he pulled her down to his chest, wanting to stay inside her as long as possible. He wasn't sure how long they remained that way until his legs cramped. Reluctantly, he pulled out of her body and rolled her to the side.

Stretching, he ensured he could stand and then went to the bathroom to get a wet washcloth. After cleaning them both, he lay back down and tucked her into his side with her head on his shoulder. Running his fingers up and down her spine, he kissed the top of her bald head. "I love you, baby."

She pressed her lips to his chest. "I love you, too." There was a pause. "Can I ask you something?"

"Anything. You should know that by now."

There was wariness in her voice. "Does it bother you that I've played with other Doms at the club? You sounded jealous of Master Carter."

Sighing, he ran his free hand down his face. "A part of me is jealous—yes, I can't deny that. But I've been in the lifestyle long enough to know play doesn't always include one's emotions. It can just be for a physical and mental release. I've never seen you emotionally invested in a scene until now, and that knowledge says you're mine. *You. Are. Mine.* Shelby. I love you. I've never said those words to a woman before—not even when I was a teenager trying to get into some girl's pants. The fact that I think those words every day around you tells me it's the real thing. I love you, Shelby, and I want to spend the rest of our lives proving it to you."

She propped herself up on her elbow and met his gaze. "I've never said those words to anyone except for Brandon Davis in the first grade, so technically, that doesn't count." A smile spread across her face when he chuckled. "I love you, too, Master. And I would love to spend the rest of our lives proving that to you."

Cuddling him once more, Shelby drifted to sleep in his arms, and he knew he'd found his reason for living. He'd been born to be hers.

CHAPTER TEN

The afternoon traffic was heavy in Boston, and Parker impatiently tapped the steering wheel, waiting for the light to turn green. Shelby reached over and touched his hand. "Your mother is going to be fine. I'm sure of it."

He twined their fingers together and kissed the back of her hand. "Thanks for coming with me. It means a lot."

"How could I not, after all you've done for me? There was no way I would sit in Florida when I could be here for you. I love you."

His heart swelled as it did every time he heard those words from her. As soon as he made sure his mother would be all right, he would pick out an engagement ring for Shelby. He wanted her to know, regardless of her test results on Friday, he wanted to marry her. For richer or poorer, in sickness and in health, she was going to be his wife if it was the last thing either one of them did on this earth.

She'd had her blood work and MRI done yesterday, right before his father's phone call about his mother's heart attack. Shelby immediately called her doctor to postpone her appointment for two days. She'd insisted on flying to Boston with him and wouldn't take no for an answer. "And I love you, too."

Ten minutes later, he pulled into his parents' development, and anxiety pooled in his gut. He never realized how much he dreaded coming home. He didn't belong here—never had. Many times, when he was growing up, he'd wondered if he'd been adopted. But, alas, his brother, father, and he shared the same birthmark on the back of their necks, and his baby picture was the spitting image of his father at that age. Thankfully, he'd only inherited physical traits from the man and not personality ones.

"These houses are huge and stunning. You grew up here?"

Parker gave her a half-hearted smile. "It had its pros and cons—with the cons being it felt like I was raised in a museum. We were never allowed to touch anything on the main floor as kids. God forbid we knocked over a fifty-thousand-dollar crystal vase."

Shelby winced. "Please don't tell me that. I'm nervous enough as it is."

Steering their rental into the long driveway to his parents' mansion, he squeezed her hand. "You'll do fine. Once we check in with my father, we'll go to the hospital to see my mother. I made hotel reservations for us nearby. I have no desire to spend any more time than necessary in this house."

He frowned as he noticed several other vehicles parked off to the side of the circular driveway. Did his father have company other than Dave? After exiting the car, Parker took Shelby's arm and led her up the stairs to the front door. He rang the bell, and she raised her eyebrows at him. "You don't have a key?"

"Hell, no. I don't want one."

The door opened, and the Christiansens' longtime British butler stood in the foyer. "Welcome, Master Parker. It's good to see you again."

Beside Parker, Shelby giggled, and he glanced at her. She brought her hand to her lips. "Sorry. I wasn't expecting the title."

He winked at her before facing the other man again, who'd stepped back to allow them to enter. "Thank you, Frederick. This is my girlfriend, Shelby Whitman."

"It's a pleasure to meet you, Miss Whitman."

Shelby stuck out her hand, catching the older man off guard. "It's nice to meet you, too, Frederick. Please, call me Shelby."

The butler shook her hand with an amused but

friendly smile. "Yes, Miss Shelby. Master Parker, your father is waiting for you in the bar room. Shall I get your bags?"

"Thanks, and no. We'll be staying at a hotel." He gave her hand a gentle tug. "Come on. Let's get this over with."

Walking through multiple opulent rooms to get where they were going, Shelby gasped and murmured, "Holy shit."

Parker snorted. "I told you, it's a fucking museum."

"You weren't kidding."

When they entered the large bar room, several things hit him at once. One—his father was laughing and joking with Mr. and Mrs. Holloway and Dave and his wife as the three men sipped scotch that cost more than five hundred dollars a bottle. Two—Cynthia Holloway smiled at him, yet appeared as if she wanted to be anywhere but in that room. But the most shocking of all was Janet Christiansen sitting in the middle of all the activity, perfectly healthy.

"Parker! Glad you could join us, son."

Anger coursing through him, his fists clenched at his father's booming voice. He was a bear of a man, having about two inches and forty pounds more on him than Parker's own frame. "Of course, I'm here. What I don't understand is what Mother is doing here when she's supposed to be in the hospital thanks to a heart attack."

Alan Christiansen stepped toward him and waved his hand nonchalantly. "Oh, that. Apparently, that was the only way to get you to visit."

"What?" he hissed. "You lied about a fucking heart attack with her knocking on death's door just to get me to drop everything and run up here?" He couldn't keep the venom from his voice. "For what? A fucking cocktail party?"

"Parker! There's no need to curse," his mother chastised as if he were still eight years old. "It was a misunderstanding."

"No, Mother. A misunderstanding is when you honestly *misunderstand* someone. In this case, it is very fucking clear there was no misunderstanding. It was a con to get me here."

Dave stood. "Calm down, Parker. What difference does it make? You're here now. Let me get you a drink."

The veins in his temples pulsated as his blood reached a boiling point. "I don't want a damn drink. I want to know what the fuck is going on."

His father raised his glass of scotch. "We're celebrating. I'm running for State Senate, and I wanted my entire family here when I announce it tomorrow. The press will be there in full force, so wear your best suit and not those jeans."

They had to be kidding him. Were there hidden cameras in the room? Was he being punked? This whole thing had been a scam so that they could pretend to be one big happy family for the fucking press?

"Oh, who's this?"

His mother's curious question had him glancing at her to figure out who she was talking about. It was at that moment he'd remembered Shelby was standing behind him, witnessing this fucked-up family reunion. With his eyes giving her a heartfelt apology, he reached for her hand and pulled her to his side. Thankfully, she seemed to forgive his brain fart. "This is my girlfriend, Shelby Whitman. Shelby, unfortunately, this is my family."

"Girlfriend?" Dave snorted and smirked. "She's a whore from that sex club you hang out at."

Parker snapped as a red haze flooded his vision. Before anyone else could react, he was across the room, tackling his brother. His fists flew as he pounded the man into a pulp. Screams and barked orders erupted from the room, but he ignored them all. Never had beating the crap out of anyone felt so fucking good.

"Parker, please stop! You have to stop! *Master*!"

It was that anguish-filled last word that penetrated his muddled brain, and he pulled his fist mid-swing, lifting his gaze to Shelby's hazel eyes. Beautiful Shelby. The woman he loved. The courageous woman who had shown him more love in the past few weeks than his family had during his entire life.

Underneath him, Dave groaned through his

swollen and bleeding lips. Shoving off the bastard, Parker stood, and Shelby rushed into his arms. He held her tightly, letting her love repair his tattered soul. "I'm sorry, baby. I'm sorry you had to be here for this."

"It's okay," she sobbed into his chest. "Let's just go."

"My thoughts exactly."

Judge Alan stepped forward, his face red with anger and disbelief. "What the hell is wrong with you, Parker? You're choosing this tramp over your own blood! You leave here now, and you can forget about ever coming back. I'll disown you."

Sneering at his sperm donor, he growled. "Too late, *Alan*. I've already disowned you. Shelby is my family now, and she's all the family I need. The rest of you can go to fucking hell."

Tucking her under his arm, he led her toward the doorway, ignoring the stuttered protests behind him. He had to get her out of there.

They were halfway down the front steps when he heard, "Parker! Parker, wait."

Ignoring the female voice, he kept walking, but Shelby glanced over her shoulder and stopped him. Spinning around, he waited as Cynthia hurried down the steps toward them. "Parker, I'm so sorry. I had no idea what was happening and that they tricked you into coming here. The only reason I came was to say hi to you. Trust me, I have no more desire to stay in that room than you do."

His shoulders relaxed a little as his old friend turned to Shelby with a smile. "Hi. I'm Cynthia. Shelby, was it?"

"Yes." She gave a tentative smile of her own.

The pretty brunette extended her hand, which Shelby shook. "It's so nice to meet you. I only wish it hadn't been this way. And I'm so sorry about the way you were treated in there. Despite our parents' insistence that we get together, Parker and I are just old friends. If it helps, they don't like my significant other either."

Snorting, Parker gave her a wry grin. "Let me guess. He's blue-collar?" Cynthia had never been the social climber many of their other friends had been.

"High-school science teacher, actually. And he's a she. Becky and I have been together a little over six months now."

Parker was stunned. He never would have guessed, but it didn't matter to him. "That's great. I'm happy for you."

"So am I. And I'm happy for you too." She glanced back at the house and adjusted the purse he hadn't noticed her carrying. "Listen. I'm not going back in there, and since, obviously, you won't be going back in there ever, would you two like to grab an early dinner? I'll call Becky and have her meet us."

He glanced at Shelby, who nodded her assent with relief in her eyes at the other woman's kind gesture. "Sounds great, Cyn. We're staying at the Boston

Harbor Hotel. Why don't we meet you in the dining room in about an hour so we can check in?"

"Perfect. Let's get away from all this high-class snobbery and make Shelby's visit to our beautiful city a fun one."

It was the best idea he'd heard all day.

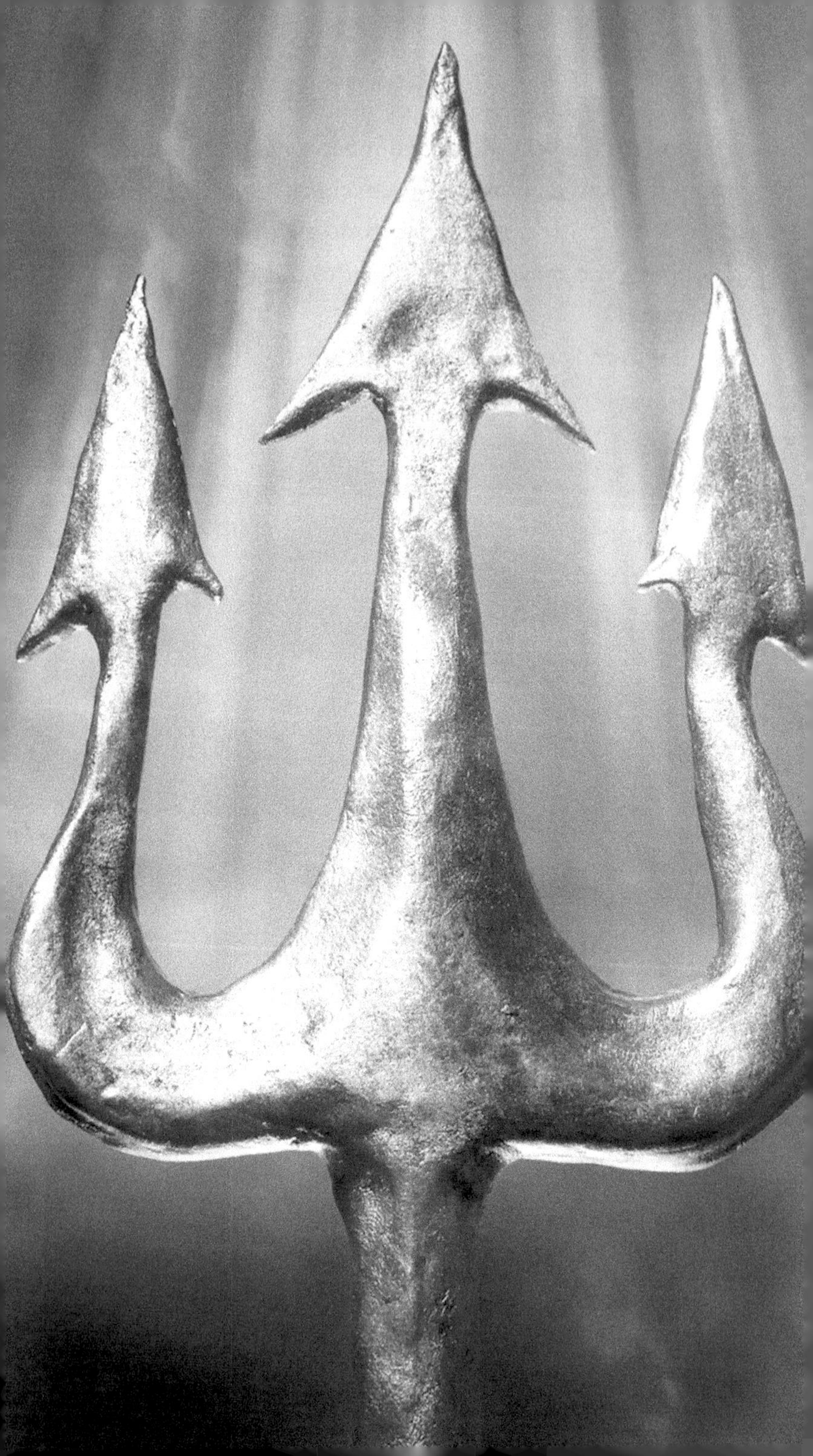

CHAPTER ELEVEN

Parker climbed back into bed after a trip to the bathroom and pulled Shelby into his arms, exactly where she belonged. His movements were cautious, letting her sleep a little longer before they had to get up and shower—hopefully together. Her doctor's appointment was in two hours, but it was only a ten-minute drive to the office.

They'd returned to Tampa yesterday afternoon after having breakfast with Cynthia and her girlfriend, Becky. The three women had gotten along terrifically the night before, and Parker invited the other couple to visit them in Florida when they had the chance. He'd been grateful they'd helped ease the horrible experi-ence from Shelby's mind.

When they had gotten home a little after four yesterday, Parker had helped Shelby into bed. She'd been exhausted but hadn't been able to sleep on the plane. After she'd dozed off, he'd called Angie and asked if she could swing by to watch her while he ran an errand, and the woman had been quick to say yes.

Shelby stirred and blinked up at him. "Hi."

"Hi, right back at you. How do you feel?"

She stretched, and her body rubbing against his made his morning wood spring back to life. "I'm good, but I need to use the bathroom."

His eyes followed her ass as she shuffled across the room to the master bath. When the door shut, he leaped out of bed and opened the top drawer of his dresser, pulling out the two boxes he'd hidden there. He was back in bed in a flash, along with Spanky, who seemed to think this was a new game. Parker pointed at his feet, and the dog got the message, lying at the foot of the bed.

Hiding the boxes under his pillow, Parker tried not to appear nervous as the bathroom door opened again, and his beautiful Shelby came out. She ran her tongue along her teeth, and he knew that indicated she'd brushed them. Over the past few weeks, he'd learned all her little quirks and habits, loving every single one of them because they were what made her unique. She scrambled back into bed and smiled when Spanky laid his big head over her ankles.

Taking her hand, Parker gazed into her eyes. In them, he saw his future. They were going to get good news today. He was sure of it. But he wanted her to know that, whether the news was good or not, he wasn't asking what he was about to ask just because her cancer was in remission.

"Baby, before we get up and dressed, I have a present for you."

Her eyes narrowed at him. "Present? What for?"

Reaching under his pillow, he pulled out the larger box and handed it to her. "Open it."

"Parker, what is it?"

He shrugged and jutted his chin toward the box sitting on her lap. She let go of his hand, opened the box, and gasped. Thankfully, it was a good gasp. "Parker, it's beautiful."

Sitting up, he lifted the gold collar embedded with a rainbow of colored gems. "I knew when I saw it that it was perfect for you. The stones will match whatever wig and outfit you want to wear to the club. And it will still be beautiful on you whether you stay bald or your hair grows back." He paused. "Actually, it will be you who makes the collar beautiful. Will you wear it, Shelby? Will you be my sub for however long we have together?"

Her eyes filled with tears as she touched his wrist. "Yes. Oh, yes. I love you, Master. For however long we have together, I'll be your sub."

Bringing the collar to her neck, he fastened the clasp at her nape, then kissed the tears on her cheek. "Shhh, baby. I have one more question for you."

She sniffled and nodded while running her fingers along the collar. Reaching under the pillow again, he pulled out the smaller box, stood, and rounded the bed to her side. Her jaw dropped when he got down on one knee and opened the lid of the box, revealing a two-carat, emerald-cut diamond ring surrounded by the same gems that were in her collar. "Now that you've agreed to be my sub, will you also agree to be my wife? I love you, Shelby. I love the children we'll adopt and raise to the best of our ability. I love the dogs we'll rescue, so Spanky has some friends to hang out with when we kick him out of the bedroom, so we don't have an audience. And I love every second of time you are by my side and in my arms where you belong. Marry me?"

In the dressing room of the church, Kristen Anders' bridesmaids and man-of-honor put the finishing touches on her dress, hair, and makeup. Then Angie pinned a single rosebud to Will's white tux lapel while Shelby handed out the women's bouquets. When Kristen took her flowers, she caught Shelby's hand. "I want you to know how happy I am that you're here with us today and will be for a long time. And don't you dare think about eloping because we already can't wait to start planning your big wedding too. Parker's a special guy, and he better know that he lucked out and got one hell of a woman."

Shelby air-kissed her cheek, so they wouldn't screw up their makeup and then grinned at the rest of the group. "I couldn't have gotten through everything without all of you. And don't worry, while we probably won't have a huge wedding, I'll still need your help planning it."

"Ladies and Will, it's time." Bill Anders stood in the doorway, dressed in his black tuxedo, staring at his daughter. "Baby, you look beautiful."

A blush bloomed on the bride's cheeks. "Thanks, Dad."

Leaving the father and daughter alone momentarily, the others hurried out to line up at the back of the church. Will was escorting Angie down the aisle since Ian, the best man, was already at the altar with the groom. Jenn had two escorts, Brody and Marco, while Kayla was walking down on Boomer's arm. Finally, Shelby was paired up with Nick, the youngest of the Sawyer brothers, who'd managed to get leave from his SEAL team in California, and Jake, the last of Kristen's Sexy Six-Pack. And damn, did they fit the moniker in their Navy dress whites, or what? She was madly in love with her Master, but she'd have to be in a coma not to notice how handsome the guys looked in their uniforms. Talk about drop-dead gorgeous.

Jake approached and kissed her lightly on the cheek. "You look great, Shelby. Love the hair."

She tugged on his small ponytail. "Love yours, too."

When they'd returned from their out-of-town assignment last week, she'd told Marco and Jake that they didn't have to shave their heads as everyone else had done. All the bald domes had been more than comical after her initial reaction, and since she was now in remission, she was ready to see everyone, including herself, return to normal. But while the other club members' hair had grown back over the past few weeks, her own was taking its damn time.

Kristen had told her to wear any one of her colored wigs, or if she wanted to, a navy scarf around her sparse peach fuzz, but Shelby hadn't wanted to take the spotlight off the bride. Parker had gone to the wig store with her the other day and helped her pick out a short hairdo a little longer than how she'd been wearing it before she got sick.

Parker. Just thinking of him had her eyes searching the crowded church for him. She couldn't wait until her doctor gave her the all-clear to resume any and all play activities because Parker was keeping things relatively vanilla until then. Once her chemo-induced anemia was gone, though, he would spank her ass for all the infractions she'd been intentionally racking up lately. And the anticipation was driving her nuts.

As the first notes of the music floated into the air, Kayla and Boomer began their walk down the aisle. Shelby and her escorts were next, and when she took that initial step, she spotted Parker at the end of a row, halfway up the aisle. He sat next to Kayla's wife, Roxy, and Kat, but his eyes were solely on her. With her hand tucked under Jake's arm, she fingered her engagement ring. She still couldn't believe she was engaged to the most wonderful man in the world.

Parker winked at her, and she smiled back, remembering what he'd told her that morning.

"Someday soon, everyone will be gathering for our wedding, baby. Then, I can spend the rest of my life making Mrs. Shelby Christiansen the happiest woman in the world. I'm going to make her laugh, smile..." He'd raised a leering eyebrow. *"And come every day. She will always know how much I love her... and that, baby, is not negotiable."*

Continue the Trident Security series with *Topping The Alpha, Trident Security Book 5* - now available.

For the best reading order of the Trident Security series and its spinoffs, check out the printable list on my website - www.samanthacolebooks.-com/pages/best-reading-order.

Want to know what's coming next? Join my Facebook Group -
Samantha Cole's Sexy Six-Pack's Sirens...

or sign up for my newsletter - samanthacolebooks.com/mailing-list

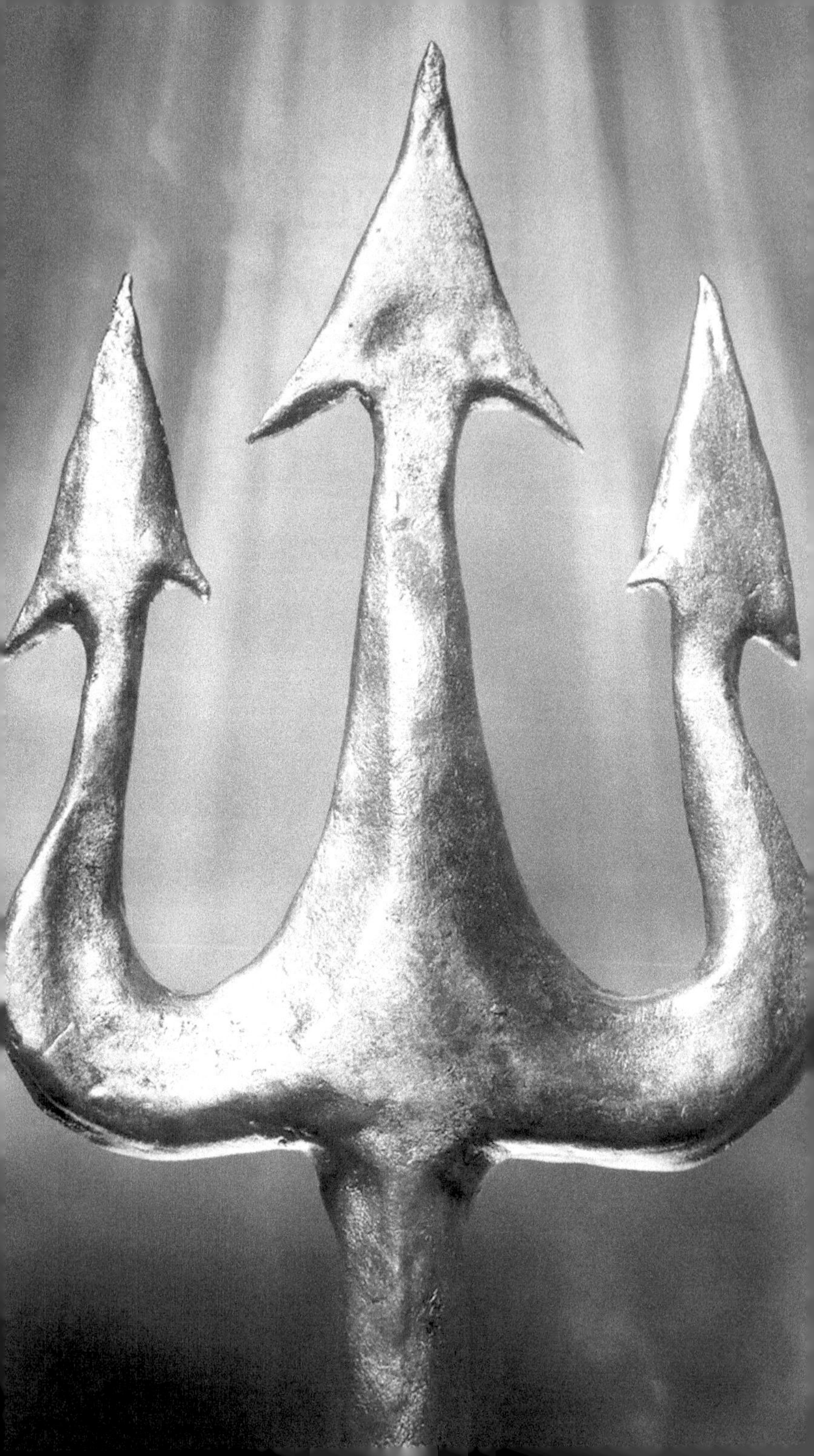

Nick Sawyer flipped on the lights and closed the door to his hotel room. Striding across the room, he unbuttoned the jacket of his Navy dress whites and tossed it on the back of a chair near the windows as he kicked off his spit-shined shoes. His brother's fiancée—now wife—had insisted the men in the bridal party wear their formal uniforms. Nick prayed when his oldest brother, Ian, got married that his future sister-in-law, Angie Beckett, agreed to elope. After years of being in combat gear, T-shirts, sweats, or jeans, dressing up in his monkey suit was irritating as hell—especially in the heat and humidity of Florida, the weekend after Labor Day.

Entering the bathroom, he pulled his white tee over his head and dropped it next to the sink, then took a piss in the toilet. He flushed and washed his hands before returning to the main room. It was oh-two-hundred hours, and he was still nicely buzzed from an evening of partying. Devon and Kristen had thrown a big shindig for their wedding, but Nick knew most, if not all, of it was Kristen's idea. Devon had collared her in a BDSM ceremony at the club he owned with Ian and would've been happy with a quickie cere-mony with one of the Tampa justices of the peace to make it legal. But his brother loved the woman, and a man in love would do anything to see his significant other happy.

Seconds after Nick flopped face-first onto the king-sized bed, there was a knock at his door, eliciting a growl from his chest. Wishing he could just yell, "Come in," he sighed and stood again to answer it, figuring it was either Ian or their dad. He turned the knob and pulled, shock punching him in the gut at the sight before him. It wasn't his brother or father. It was Jake. Jake Donovan—his brothers' teammate in the SEALs and now in their operative business, Trident Security. Otherwise known by his nickname from the Navy—Reverend. And, fuck, the man was hot. As uncomfortable as Nick had been in his dress uniform, Jake looked completely at ease in his. And hot. Had he mentioned that already?

"Hey." Was that all he could say to the sexy-as-sin man standing before him?

He watched as Jake's emerald-green eyes traveled downward, taking in Nick's bare chest, sculpted abs, open belt buckle, and everything below it. His breath hitched as the man's intense gaze returned to his face, and his cock began to swell at the heat he saw there.

"Mind if I come in?"

Holy shit! Nick knew exactly what Jake was asking. It was what he'd been fantasizing about all night. Him... Jake... together. *Holy shit!* "Um, yeah."

He took a step to the side and opened the door wider. As Jake brushed past him, Nick inhaled deeply, and his cock twitched against the material of his pants. The man smelled incredible—like a forest, fresh from a morning rain, combined with a hint of leather—and Nick wondered what cologne it was.

Letting out a long exhale, he shut the door before turning around and...

Fuck! Jake was lying on his side along the bottom of the bed with his head propped up in his hand. Posing like that, he could be modeling for a magazine. He certainly had the body for it, and the only thing marring his beautiful, sculpted face was a small scar next to his left eye, but it only enhanced his good looks. The top two buttons of Jake's white dress coat were undone, revealing the collar of his T-shirt and a few light strands of chest hair. Nick's mouth watered as his legs became weak.

What was it about this man which made him want to drop to his knees and beg? Nick had always been the alpha in every relationship he'd had since he joined the Navy at eighteen, but Jake had him yearning to submit in every way. He knew all about the BDSM club his brothers owned and that Jake was a member of. He'd even been inside a few times and cleared to play, but he never did... play, that is.

It wasn't as if he hadn't seen any guy he could get interested in because there had been a few good-looking men who'd caught his eye. What was holding him back was that he didn't quite understand the draw to the lifestyle, and he also hadn't come out to his family yet. And hooking up at The Covenant was not how he wanted to do it.

He knew his parents and brothers would have no problem with him being gay, so why he hadn't come out to them was a question he kept asking himself. But with Jake Donovan in his hotel room, with blatant desire in his eyes, Nick didn't give a shit about anything else at the moment.

"I was..." He cleared his throat. "I was just getting ready for bed."

Shit, that sounded so fucking lame. *Get a grip, Sawyer.*

"Really? Then don't let me stop you. Please continue."

The whiskey-laced voice sent shivers down Nick's spine, and he didn't move a muscle. He knew Jake was ordering him to undress, but he was being held in place by his penetrating stare. Those eyes seemed to delve straight into his soul, trying to figure out what made him tick, nonetheless still hiding the man's own secrets behind a shroud. Swallowing hard, Nick crossed his right arm over his chest and grabbed the opposite elbow. It was a defensive yet unsure stance, and he watched as Jake's pupils widened in unadulterated lust. Nick felt like a sheep being eyed by a hungry wolf, and his breathing and pulse rates increased. "I... um..."

He didn't know what to say. He wanted this man in the worst way, and he was sure the feeling was mutual. They'd been avoiding each other all night, but their eyes had met hundreds of times over the last ten hours or so. It had been a few years since they'd seen each other. Since SEAL Team Three was based in Coronado, California, Nick hadn't had many opportunities to get to Tampa. On the few occasions he'd made the trip to the Sunshine State, Jake had been out of town on different assignments each time. Nick had arrived in Florida two days ago and been floored by the hunk when they first saw each other at the bachelor party later that night. He'd always thought the guy was good-looking, but the sudden attraction, which had hit Nick over the head this time, was stronger than anything he'd ever felt.

Jake was four inches taller than Nick's six-foot-one and, at about two-ten, had around fifteen pounds more muscle—in fact, lean, sinewy muscle would be a more accurate description. His medium-brown hair was a little longer than Nick remembered, and he longed to run his fingers through it to see if it was as silky as it looked. At the party the other night, held at

Donovan's, a pub owned by Jake's brother, the man had sported a two-day growth of whiskers on his chiseled face. He'd since shaved for the wedding, and Nick wasn't sure which way he preferred because both were sexy as hell.

He flinched when Jake leaped from the bed and stalked toward him—the wolf had morphed into a panther, but the same hunger was displayed in his eyes. The man hadn't missed the involuntary jerk, and an evil grin spread across his handsome face. How long had Nick been standing there staring? Seconds? Minutes? Eons? He retreated until his back hit the wall, and there was nowhere else to go—not that he wanted to escape. *Hell, no!*

Jake bit his lower lip, his gaze roaming Nick's face. "Let me help you finish getting ready."

Praying he wouldn't embarrass himself, Nick almost came in his boxer briefs when the man's hand reached for the open belt buckle and pushed it out of the way. An arm crossed his chest and held him prisoner against the wall. All he could do was clench his fists as they hung heavy at his sides while boiling blood surged through his veins. The rich, smoky scent of Jack Daniel's Single Barrel hit his nose. However, Jake showed no signs of intoxication—well, maybe he was a little buzzed, but no more than Nick.

Jake's face moved closer, and Nick licked his lips in anticipation. He felt the zipper of his pants being lowered over his throbbing erection, and once again, he prayed he wouldn't come prematurely. That hadn't happened since he was fifteen, and he sure as hell didn't want it happening now. Not with this man. Puffs of breath caressed his mouth and chin when Jake stopped inches from where Nick wanted him.

"You ready to be topped, little boy? Because I'm going to dominate you, and you'll submit to my every whim."

Nick stiffened and tilted his chin in defiance. "I'm not a boy." He wished he'd also added that he wasn't a submissive, but the Dom before him wouldn't have believed him anyway. This man was the only person who'd ever made him feel submissive, made him want and need in ways he'd never known, and he unsuccessfully fought the feeling in his gut.

"Tonight, you are. Tonight, you're *my boy,* and I'm going to fuck *my boy* any way I want."

Nick never had a chance to respond as Jake's mouth came down hard against his and...

"Sir? Excuse me, sir?"

Shaking his head, Nick opened his eyes to see the blonde-haired, first-class stewardess staring at him. He glanced down quickly and was relieved to see the book he'd been reading was open on his lap and hiding his painful erection. He looked back up with a sheepish expression. "I'm sorry. What did you say?"

She gave him a thousand-watt smile which he was sure had heterosexual males drooling over her. It did nothing for him. "We're getting ready to land, sir. Please put your seat and tray table up."

Nick reached for the lever and sat forward, wincing as his jeans tightened further in the crotch. The memory of that incredible night two months ago faded away, and he wondered what Jake would say when he saw him again. He was on a four-week leave, and instead of visiting his parents and old friends in Norfolk, Virginia, he'd decided to take a chance and spend the time off in Florida. He hoped he was doing the right thing.

Topping The Alpha: Trident Security Book 5 is now available!

Getting involved with your brothers' friend and employee is never a good idea...

After relinquishing control to Jake Donovan for one night, Nick Sawyer wants more. Nick's past as a Navy SEAL has made him a take-charge kind of guy in every relationship he's ever had, but now he finds himself craving to submit to Jake again.

The problem is Jake's determination that it will never

happen. But Nick starts breaking through Jake's defenses when they're thrown together to help a girl in danger. And their chemistry burns a bond between them.

When things go awry, can Jake confront the ghosts of his past before they steal his future?

OTHER BOOKS BY SAMANTHA COLE

******* Denotes titles/series that are only available on select digital sites. Paperbacks and audiobooks are available on most book sites.

THE TRIDENT SECURITY SERIES

Leather & Lace

His Angel

Waiting For Him

Not Negotiable

Topping The Alpha (MM)

Watching From the Shadows

Whiskey Tribute

Tickle His Fancy

No Way in Hell: A Steel Corp/Trident Security Crossover (co-authored with J.B. Havens)

Absolving His Sins

Option Number Three (MMF)

Salvaging His Soul

Trident Security Field Manual

Torn In Half

Burning For Him

*****Heels, Rhymes, & Nursery Crimes Series**

(with 13 other authors)

Jack Be Nimble: A Trident Security-Related Short Story

*****The Deimos Series**

Handling Haven: Special Forces: Operation Alpha

Cheating the Devil: Special Forces: Operation Alpha

The Trident Security Omega Team Series

Mountain of Evil

A Dead Man's Pulse

Forty Days & One Knight

The Doms of The Covenant Series

Double Down & Dirty (MFM)

Entertaining Distraction

Knot a Chance

Finding His Forever (MM)

Reclaiming His Soulmate

The Blackhawk Security Series

Tuff Enough

Blood Bound

Master Key Series

Master Key Resort

Master Cordell

HAZARD FALLS SERIES

Don't Fight It (MMF)

Don't Shoot the Messenger (MFM)

Don't Burn Bridges

THE MALONE BROTHERS SERIES

Her Secret

Her Sleuth

Her Savior

LARGO RIDGE SERIES

Cold Feet

***ANTELOPE ROCK SERIES
(CO-AUTHORED WITH J.B. HAVENS)

Wannabe in Wyoming

Wistful in Wyoming (M/M)

COCK & BULL SERIES (M/M)

Scout

Rico

STANDALONES

Where the Broken Bloom

Scattered Moments in Time: A Collection of Short Stories & More

Sweet Revenge

The Sugarplum Fairy (M/M)

*****THE BID ON LOVE SERIES**

(WITH 7 OTHER AUTHORS!)

Going, Going, Gone: Book 2

*****THE COLLECTIVE: SEASON TWO**

(WITH 7 OTHER AUTHORS!)

Angst: Book 7 (M/M)

SPECIAL COLLECTIONS

Trident Security Series: Volume I

Trident Security Series: Volume II

Trident Security Series: Volume III

Trident Security Series: Volume IV

Trident Security Series: Volume V

Trident Security Series: Volume VI

ABOUT SAMANTHA COLE

USA Today Bestselling Author Samantha Cole is a retired police officer and paramedic who now writes heart-pounding romance in multiple forms—MF, MM, and ménage. From military heroes to rugged cowboys and small-town heat, her stories blend passion, loyalty, and danger in perfect balance.

Awards:

Wannabe in Wyoming (co-authored by J.B. Havens) won the bronze medal in the 2021 Readers' Favorite Awards in the General Romance category.

Scattered Moments in Time won the gold medal in the 2020 Readers' Favorite Awards in the Fiction Anthology category.

Where the Broken Bloom (formerly *The Road to Solace*) won the silver medal in the 2017 Readers' Favorite Awards in the Contemporary Romance category.

Sexy Six-Pack's Sirens Group on Facebook
Website: www.samanthacolebooks.com
Newsletter: samanthacolebooks.com/mailing-list

facebook.com/SamanthaColeAuthor

instagram.com/samanthacoleauthor

bookbub.com/profile/samantha-a-cole

goodreads.com/SamanthaCole

amazon.com/Samantha-A-Cole/e/B00X53K3X8

tiktok.com/@samanthacoleauthor

youtube.com/@SamanthaACole-bp6yu

ACKNOWLEDGMENTS

To the fans of the Trident Security Series—you'll find that Shelby and Parker's story is a little different from the other books in the series. There is no one shooting at them, or trying to kidnap them for any reason, but they do have their struggles. I hope you enjoy reading their story as much as I enjoyed writing it. Thanks for asking for more stories about my characters. It is because of you that I continue to write them.

To Tori and Bullmastiff Rescue, Inc. for helping to bring Spanky into this story.

To my editor, Eve Arroyo, for being a pleasure to work with.

As always, thanks to my Beta-readers and friends who've help make this book the best it can be.

*****

Keep reading for a preview of
Topping the Alpha: Trident Security Book 5

www.ingramcontent.com/pod-product-compliance
Lightning Source LLC
Chambersburg PA
CBHW060751210726
48292CB00014B/2760